the touch

Patricia
Hickman

THE
TOUCH

based on the painting by
Ron DiCianni

Tyndale House Publishers. Inc.. Wheaton. Illinois

Visit Tyndale's exciting Web site at www.tyndale.com

Designed by Dean H. Renninger

Edited by Sue Lerdal

Published in association with the literary agency of Alive Communications, Inc., 7680 Goddard Street, Suite 200, Colorado Springs, CO 80920.

This novella is a work of fiction. Names, characters, places, and incidents are either the product of the author's imagination or are used fictitiously. Any resemblance to actual events, locales, organizations, or persons living or dead is entirely coincidental and beyond the intent of either the author or publisher.

Library of Congress Cataloguing-in-Publication Data

07 06 05 04 03 02
9   8   7   6   5   4   3   2   1

acknowledgments

Thank you to Pastor Nivan Fields, who was generous with providing facts about the setting for the New Orleans Mission as well as offering an insider's perspective about running a homeless shelter. Also, thanks so much to the Tyndale editors Becky Nesbitt, Jan Stob, and Sue Lerdal for your patience, prayers, and guidance as we shaped this story with purpose and wonder. You ladies are the personification of humility. Your vision for excellence is secondary only to the light of Christ that shines out of you. One never knows what life will throw one's way. I'm so glad to find myself surrounded by such great friends on days when I desperately need someone to hold my hand and provide the healing touch of Christ in a tangible way. To the family of Tyndale House Publishing, you are truly His hands extended, but the greatest news of all is that you are my friends. And to Greg, my agent, who helps me keep my center and tolerates the annoying little threads in my peculiar patchwork fabric. Greg, you are the best.

dedication

To Ken Hickman, the steadiest ship in the fleet. God makes men like you to calm the trembling hearts and speak sense into the fray. I am proud to call you my father-in-law.

She had heard about Jesus, so she came up behind him
through the crowd and touched the fringe of his robe. For she thought
to herself, "If I can just touch his clothing, I will be healed."

MARK 5:27-28, NLT

1

IT NEVER SNOWED in New Orleans in winter.

The sky filled with the same darkness found inside the deepest
part of a cold, damp cave, and although occasionally the temperatures dropped low enough to warrant a token fire in the fireplace,
the clouds over Louisiana seldom squeezed out a single flake of
snow. The best description that Sydney Oliver could offer The Big
Easy in winter was "plainly miserable."

If it rained, it flooded, and the entire city became a concrete
swamp. The dead were buried aboveground in cemetery vaults just
to keep them in their place.

Sydney stooped partially inside the cramped telephone booth
to button the sweater on her five-year-old son, Trevor, who stood
holding the hand of his little sister, Allie. The nearby shopping

center bustled with the post-Thanksgiving, pre-Christmas shoppers, while a rusted speaker squeaked out store commercials between intermittent strains of "Silent Night."

"Are we going home yet, Mommy?" Trevor asked.

"Not yet, honey." Sydney kissed the top of his head. The soft, wet tendrils of his hair felt sticky against her lips. Then she turned and attempted to force the booth door closed. But it creaked open again as the blustery wind invaded their tiny shelter.

"Are you calling Daddy?" Trevor persisted.

Trevor's questions had not ceased since they had fled from their small rental apartment after breakfast. She deposited a handful of coins into the pay phone. "No, Trevor. We won't be calling Daddy for a while."

She held her fingers over the dialing pad but hesitated. The gold band on her ring finger had lost its sheen. Her left hand curled into a fist as she placed her head against the wall of the phone booth. She couldn't crumple now, she told herself, and chastened herself for feeling weak. Trevor and Allie had to be her greatest concern. Once more she reached to dial the number she dreaded calling. But again she froze as she saw her own image in the silver chrome frame of the pay phone.

I can't let Dad and Mother know about it. Shame swept through her, along with remorse. The battered area around her right eye had swollen and turned black. But her mind must have been in instinctive overdrive. Her fingers began to dial.

Sydney Oliver rarely broke under the weight of defeat. Growing up in a pastor's home had long ago toughened her coping mechanisms, she felt. So when she relayed stories of her childhood, she admitted only those details that painted her in the most triumphal light. But as she reached to phone her father for the second time this morning, the very act conjured up the things that she hated most about herself.

One remembrance in particular echoed from the stagnant wells of her past. Invoking the memory always made her feel like a six-year-old again—just as calling her father right now made her feel like a loser. She recalled the Sunday her father had been inducted as pastor of a church in Tennessee. It was a small, friendly congregation. But the congregational custom had required that her entire family stand up in front of the pulpit as the members passed by to greet each of them. Sydney had felt so small, so terrified. Her older brother, Lance, had stood next to her and soaked up all of the attention. But the ceremony of it all had caused a huge lump in her throat. Anxiety seethed inside of her and spilled out in the form of tears. She had felt ashamed.

Seated in the front row with her mother and brother, Sydney had initially felt a complete sense of well-being as her father delivered the morning's message. No one had warned her that she would soon be asked to rise and approach the platform as one hundred and sixty onlookers examined her with their stares. When her father had called the family forward, she had remained in her seat, paralyzed by fear. Finally, after several verbal attempts to wedge her from her place, her father, Pastor Wade Jenkins, had stepped down and taken her by the hand. Normally the gesture would have comforted her. But on that anxious morning, she could not be consoled by normal means. At that moment, she had clutched the hem of his coat. She clung to it, desperate, feeling misunderstood by her entire family. She had remained with her fist tightly curled around her father's coattail until the last member had patted her head and passed her by. Once, she had gambled and glanced up at him. But then she had looked away, not wanting to read the disappointment in his face.

Shamed later by her brother, Sydney had never forgotten the desperate feeling of that moment. But in no way could it compare with the desperation of this past hour.

"Hello, thank you for calling Clearwater Freewill. How may I direct your call?"

"Carol, please," she said.

"May I ask who's calling?"

Sydney's lips parted, but no sensible words emerged—nothing that would pass for normal conversation anyway. The wind now slammed hard drops of rain against the phone booth. Trevor tried to lead his sister in the Christmas chorus that blasted from the shopping center.

"Hello? This is Carol. Anyone there?"

"Carol, this is Sydney—"

"Sydney, dear, how are you? We so enjoyed your visit last summer. And those children are so precious—"

"Carol, I—" Sydney heard her own voice break, felt the next wave of tears tumble down her cheeks. Four-year-old Allie tugged at the loose denim around her knees.

"Whatever is the matter, dear?"

All Sydney could muster was a meager, "I need to talk to my dad."

She heard the familiar click of Carol placing the line on hold, followed by the recorded message that told of the church's upcoming Christmas celebration.

"Sing, Mommy. *All is calm, all is bright . . .*"

"Oh, Trevor, not now, honey."

"Holy infaso tender and mild. Sleep in heavenly pe-eace, sleep in heavenly peace."

Sydney's lashes lifted, and she saw a red economy car head toward them. It slowed. She dropped the phone in panic. A wet blast of wind whistled in through the partially open door, and Allie shrieked.

"Trevor, take Mommy's hand. We need to run!" She scooped Allie into her arms and cradled the child's small, wind-chapped face against herself.

"Run again, Mommy?"

"Yes, baby," she said to her son. "Run fast, okay?"

"No, Mommy. Pick me up, please?"

Trevor's short, plump arms reached up toward her. His bottom lip quivered, and Sydney realized that he sensed her anxiety. She lifted him onto her other hip and braced herself to face the squall.

Sydney staggered with them out into the hostile storm, three urban refugees trying to look invisible. The rain pelted against them, a swirling dance that mocked the trio.

The dangling phone receiver buzzed with the voice that called out, unanswered. It sounded almost mechanical against the background din of the holiday carol. *Holy night, all is calm . . .*

"Sydney, this is Daddy . . . you there, sweetie? Sydney?"

2

"PERSONAL CALL on line two, Pastor."

"Who is it?"

"They wouldn't give me a name."

The first line flashed in time to the Christmas twinkle lights in Pastor Wade Jenkins's window. Wade sighed. He wanted to resign from his church every Christmas. He entered the season lean, his weight finally five pounds shy of last year's indulgences from the gift tins given to him between Thanksgiving and Christmas—offerings of coconut-encrusted fruit, cookies matted with macadamia and raisins, and golf ball–shaped chocolates—all of the frippery somehow shoved into spray-painted baskets or coffee mugs inscribed with phrases such as "A Prayer for the Shepherd." His wife, Isabella, now boasted a collection of fifty inspirational coffee mugs, none of which she could dispense with in the yearly church bazaar for fear of repercussions from the flock.

Carol Beaman, Pastor Wade Jenkins's secretary, buzzed a second call through in spite of his rule against it. "Have them call me back—no, take a message, Carol. Sorry, Frank. These phones are going nuts. 'Tis the season." Frank Hawkins, another pastor across town, had called only to brag about his Monday golf score. Jenkins had not seen the green himself in six months.

"I should go. Bye, Frank . . . No . . . Maybe in January." Jenkins propped his feet atop the middle joist beneath his desk and pressed the small of his spine against his chair back. The roller-legged affair, designed for a thinner man with a keen penchant for computers, shifted the slightest hair of a space—just enough to cause a sharp pinch in his hindquarters.

His intercom buzzed again.

"Would now be a good time to come in, sir?" Carol had a timid voice that climbed her timorous syllables in a high pitch, sliding down her words until it reached the dead finish line of her sentences. Even over the intercom, her voice pooled in the culvert of her insecurities.

"I want a new chair, Carol."

"Want me to put that in the notes for the improvements committee meeting, sir?"

"Sure." He'd like to see the committee actually vote something in.

"Sir?"

"Did you need something, Carol?"

"May I come in, Pastor?"

Pastor. The title weighed heavily on Jenkins this time of year. If

8

he had heard it once, he had heard it at least fifty thousand times over the last few weeks. The sound of his own name now wearied him and left him feeling sour. By the time Christmas truly arrived, he would see it rehearsed twenty-two times, sprayed with sixty-five cans of glittering gold paint, trampled underfoot by a dozen borrowed farm animals and thirty little boys dragged against their will onto a hay-strewn stage. And all for the purpose of capturing a capricious audience that would darken their doors only once this year—maybe twice, if the Easter musical had the budget to draw them inside.

"Sure, come in." Jenkins raked a hand through his thin auburn-and-gray hair. As he waited for his secretary to enter with her usual overriding list of requests, he examined the advertising portfolio that lay across his walnut desk—the only piece of old furniture he could not replace because it had been handmade by a church founder. The art department, in his estimation, had done a bang-up job on the layout and advertising copy for the Christmas extravaganza. But Jenkins sighed at the thought of the Christmas tide that would soon crash down upon him. While the Tampa Bay area geared up for winter tourists by coiling red-and-green blinking Christmas lights around the trunks of palm trees, the church wound its life around pageants and musicals and magi with bad accents—anything that would draw a crowd.

The door opened as he slipped into his dark suit jacket. The sound of canned Christmas instrumentals followed Carol into the room.

"Pastor Jenkins, two things. First off, Grace Huddleston says her daughter, Suzie, needs to move up the wedding date."

"Suzie . . . the Suzie I've been counseling for the last month?"

"Yes, Suzie and Buzz."

"Don't young people look younger nowadays?"

"I wouldn't say that."

"Suzie wants to move up the date. Wonder what Buzz says about that?"

"Grace says it's a hurried ceremony. But she won't talk to anyone but you about it, she says."

"I'll check the calendar. She knows it's almost Christmas?"

"Grace insists that you do it, Pastor. Sounds a little anxious, if you catch my drift?"

"Have Grace call me, then."

"Will do. Also, Nora wants to know if you want red or green paper for the Sunday circular."

"What was that?" Jenkins made a more honest attempt to focus on Carol's words.

Carol held up two reams of paper, one red and one green. She stood posed like Moses on Sinai while she awaited his decision.

"Carol, will you please tell Nora, for once, she can pick the color herself?"

Nora Maggert had headed up the ladies' volunteer bulletin-stuffing brigade for fifteen years. Many believed that if the job had been absorbed into the now substantial secretarial pool, Nora would have ceased to exist. She was the bulletin-stuffing countess supreme, and she reminded all who chanced to pass her way on Sunday mornings about her every-Friday burden for the Lord.

"She's so old, it's best to humor her. Besides, Nora loves it when you offer your opinion, Pastor."

"All right, then, green."

Carol hefted the green one, then paused. The hesitation reflected from her brown eyes.

"You like the red, Carol?"

"It's a stronger color, don't you think?"

"Red, then. May I get back to work, or does Nora want me to come and pick out what she's eating for lunch today?"

"You would do that?"

Jenkins drummed his desktop and calculated the exact amount of silence needed to chase Carol from the room.

"Oh, and did you take that last call?" she asked.

He stared at the phone. Line two's red light was dim.

"Maybe whoever it was will call back." She bustled out.

An early-afternoon fatigue settled upon him. Unable to analyze any further, he gathered the advertising campaign material into his soft leather briefcase. He would study it once more after dinner tonight at home. He massaged his throat and sipped the last dregs of hot, black coffee.

"Carol?" He spoke into the telephone intercom.

"Yes, sir?"

"Have you seen my cough drops? I've got a throat tickle that's driving me crazy."

"Cough drops? Were they packaged in cute little wrappers with fruit stamped on the sides?"

"Sounds right."

"I thought it was Christmas candy. I'm sorry. I shook them out into a dish, and—wait. I see them. There are two left and—"

"Never mind." He reached to punch the Off button but first said, "No more calls for a while, please."

His early lunch with the church board had drained him. Frank Hazzleby, the head elder, scheduled meetings to plan other meetings. When Wade had accepted the pastorship of Clearwater Freewill

11

Tabernacle over five years ago, he had inherited a long-standing board of elders whose family memberships dated back as far as three generations. So did some of their ideals.

Clearwater Freewill, a church highly respected in the community, had once held a membership of over a thousand. And if the truth were revealed, the records yet reflected the same rosters. But somehow over the years the growth had stagnated—along with the truth about the rosters. Holding high its proud banner, the church and its traditions raged on with all the fury of an Arctic blizzard. In the last three decades, five pastors had marched into its portals and then out again. Jenkins was holy man number six. But instead of starting with a new, clear vision, Jenkins had been handed the position as he would have been given a rusted baton and told to run the same race in the same rut of another man's tracks. Instead of assuming the duties of a pastor, he felt more like a Christmas ghost haunting the hallowed corridors of a pristine museum.

"Pastor Jenkins, you've got a call on line one. It's the call we lost from a while ago."

The sound of Carol's voice made him heave a sigh. "I asked you to hold all calls."

"But, sir, this is important—"

"Carol, you'll take a message for me, then. I've got to go over these budget figures before Monday's year-end meeting."

A long silence followed.

"Did you hear me?"

"I did, sir. But you'd best take this call. It's your daughter, Sydney. She's crying, sir."

3

"ONLY SIX DOLLARS? We paid thirty for that ring." Sydney pulled Allie closer. A Rottweiler padded out from behind the pawnshop counter. His eyes locked on Allie. Trevor squatted next to a glass case and pointed at open cartons of yo-yos.

"Gold is volatile right now, miss. They've overregulated the whole metals industry." He read her confusion. "You buy high, you sell low."

"Maybe I'll try another pawnshop." The pawnshop owner made no effort to meet her bluff with a higher offer. When the taxi driver had dropped them off at the corner, she hadn't noticed any other pawnbrokers in the area. From outside, she had paraded back and forth for fifteen minutes before mustering the courage to walk into the dim shop.

The broker lit one cigarette with another and used his coffee cup for an ashtray. "Lady, I get these gold wedding bands all the time." The pawnbroker lifted a cardboard box from a shelf. He shook it in front of her. "You want a return on your investment, you buy something with stones in it. I'll do this for you; if you buy something, trade up, maybe in the swap I could give you a little more."

"But I don't want another ring. Just the cash."

The shop owner's wife appeared, a slow-moving woman with red hair pulled back into a barrette. "Your little girl's a cutie. Looks like my granddaughter, Brandy. Honey, you want a cookie?"

Before Sydney could tell her no, Allie reached for the cookie.

"Let her have one or two, Mom. I just bought six boxes of these cookies last night from my niece. School project or some such. If I eat all of these, I'll need a forklift just to carry me home."

Allie took the cookies from Mrs. Pawnbroker.

"So you're selling your wedding band." The wife studied Sydney's face. "You think maybe you'll be coming back for this ring later?"

Sydney shook her head. "No, ma'am."

"Fred, what are you trying to do? You need to clean your glasses. I'll give you twenty dollars for this ring," she said.

"Doris, that ring's not worth twenty."

"It is to me. I know my jewelry. I got a twenty on me. I'll buy it myself." Doris opened an old snap purse. She pulled a crisp twenty from a zipper pocket. She handed it to Sydney. "Sold."

Sydney watched Doris tuck the ring where the twenty once lay hidden. She turned to tell Trevor to back away from the Rottweiler. It lapped at his forehead. She saw herself in a rusted metal mirror used for customers who tried on jewelry. Around her eye, the swollen dark bruise looked worse than it did this morning. "I just want what it's worth. Let me give you some change."

"Sorry, I got a beauty appointment. Got to run." Doris clutched the purse next to her.

"Pick me up one of those grinders, babe," Fred said.

Sydney detected his New Jersey accent and the fact that he called po' boys "grinders."

He watched Doris leave. "My babe, she's stubborn. Once she gets something in her head, she won't listen to nobody. You keep the twenty. Here's a coupon for two dollars off at Bud's Deli to boot." He pressed the coupon into her hand.

"I don't know what to say—thank you. Trevor, let's go."

"I like your dog, mister," Trevor said.

"Some people are afraid 'cause Butch, he's a Rottweiler. But he's a good dog."

"Looks can be deceiving." Sydney paused to offer Fred the Pawnbroker a smile. "You tell Doris she's an angel."

"I tell her that all the time. She doesn't listen. Maybe she'll listen this time."

Sydney led the kids out into the spitting rain.

"SORRY, I CAN'T TALK NOW, Sam. I'm waiting for a call." Jenkins felt cold inside and the chill swelled as though it were an expanse between himself and his grown daughter in Louisiana. He could see her two children, waiflike faces with eyes almond brown, so close in age some mistook Trevor and Allie for twins until

Trevor turned five. They both had their mother's dark auburn hair. Sydney never finished college, intent on motherhood. Jenkins always imagined his grandparent season differently. Sydney would finish school, he imagined, to marry a peer, an *intellectual equal*. After a few years of establishing herself in finance, motherhood would come. Someone had reshuffled the deck.

Isabella reminded Wade often of how anxious he had been to marry her, of how they struggled to buy simple essentials while he finished seminary. Why the good Lord gave women such exhaustive memories, he would never know.

"We don't expect you to memorize the entire narrative, Pastor. But, if you don't mind my saying so, if you could know it well enough that you're not staring down at the script so much, it would help us a great deal. Our last pastor never took much time out for the Christmas pageant and, well, it showed," said the music director, Sam Farris. Sam paced in front of Jenkins's desk, obviously nervous about the upcoming musical although he had directed the same production for ten years.

"What about Charlie Weaver, Sam? He's a gifted orator," said Jenkins.

"It's never been done that way here at Clearwater Freewill. The congregation expects the pastor to narrate."

"You've never said, Sam—who started the custom?"

"Pastors inspire people. Christmas should be about inspiring."

He watched while Sam Farris disappeared over to the manger scene that Isabella had arranged on his bookcase. Sam's Christmas production had been in full swing a year prior to when Wade took the pastorate. The music minister had struck him as a nervous sort, and colorless, especially around the eyes. But once the final hallelujah had been sung and the manger put away until the day it would be dragged out again eleven months later, a calm had settled upon Sam and the music department. Until Easter, of course.

"I'd like to see laypeople take more platform duties. It's good for them. The Christmas pageant's a good way to start," Wade said.

"Why don't I leave the script here with you? You'll let me know if you think we need to change anything? You know, for instance, if a phrase doesn't sound like something you'd say. We want our narrative to sound authentic."

"I'd venture to say none of it sounds like me, Sam. The script is twenty years old."

"Just use your best judgment, Pastor."

Jenkins's gaze followed a dark band of clouds. The pregnant billows darkened the sunlight outside his window. "They say a storm's moving in from the southwest. Supposed to get cooler. Might even need to pull out a jacket in the morning." He fingered the script. The sky lost all color. "Think we'll get snow this year, Sam?"

"In Florida, Pastor? It'll snow in Tampa Bay the same year the church cancels Christmas pageants."

"Wouldn't *that* be the end of the world?"

Sam laughed.

Carol's voice broke in from the intercom. "Your wife is calling, Pastor."

"Any word from Sydney, Carol?"

Carol said no.

"I should take this call, Farris. Family matter."

"Just one more thing. Rehearsals have already started. So your presence might encourage the cast if you could come, say, a few times each week?"

"Please, Sam, have Charlie Weaver stand in for me. I'll come for the dress rehearsal. You have my word."

"Won't you need more practice, Pastor?"

"Sam, let's try and meet again. The Christmas pageant will turn out fine. It always does."

"Can we discuss this in the staff meeting?" Farris bundled the Christmas scripts beneath one arm.

"No, sorry. The itinerary is too full. See you in five, though. Staff meeting." He waited while the music director disappeared behind the large oak door. He picked up the receiver. "Isabella, have you heard from Sydney?"

"Wade, what's going on? I was out when she called. She sounded like she was crying."

"Carol thought so too."

"I was hoping you had the chance to speak with her."

"She hung up. I didn't have a chance. Have you tried reaching her in-laws?"

"They don't know anything. As usual. Neither of them will admit that Ray, well, that he—"

"Don't talk to them about Ray. You know it never does any good. Approach them from the standpoint of the grandchildren."

"You talk to them, Wade. I don't know what to say. I get all fuzzled."

"Did Sydney's message tell you where she is?"

"Only that she and Ray had another argument and that she and the kids had to leave the apartment. I don't know what to think about it all, Wade, except I think she's on the run." Isabella's tone sounded breathy, as though the last thin thread of oxygen ebbed from her.

"Don't jump to conclusions. I have a staff meeting in five minutes. Can't you try and call the apartment again?"

"I'll keep trying. But I'm at my wit's end, Wade. What if he finds them? Shouldn't we call the police?"

"And tell them what? We don't know enough, Izz."

"You should hear her tone, Wade, just like she gets when she's upset. Her voice is all volatile, and I can distinguish when she's volatile."

"Vulnerable?"

"She's in trouble. I know my Sydney."

"She'll call again, honey. Sydney's a smart girl." *In theory, anyway.*

Isabella hung up. The dial tone buzzed metrically, but Wade scarcely noticed how long he sat with the receiver to his ear staring out at the gray sky. Isabella's fright seeped inside him. Her consoling voice had touched him like a lifeline on many afternoons. He remembered days when troubles thwarted him, left him unable to piece together a lucid sentence. Isabella cheered him on and walked beside him until the light broke through. But today her tone was irregular, emptied of all rational thought.

"Pastor," Carol's voice crackled across the intercom, "I have your staff report ready, sir."

Wade told her to bring it on in but later would not recall her coming or going or how she slid the leather folio beneath his fingertips. The pastoral staff members trickled in and took seats around the long executive table. Poise and authority took rightful sentry on Wade's face. But he didn't feel pastorly today. It occurred to him that he would never stop being a father. The day Sydney was placed into his hands—pink, frail arms flailing as she sucked in those first few breaths only to expel her gulp of air in a newborn protest—he broke in two. The pain was agonizing and wonderful and was lodged, a clumsy tenant, inside the armor of his manhood. He thought the ache would lift from his heart and life would restore itself to bliss and he would feel young again. Adolescence forgot to wave good-bye. Now they were a family of four. *Here's your diploma, Jenkins, and your college bills, oh, and a tiny, helpless daughter.*

"Coffee, sir?" Wade's youth pastor, Loren Matthews, tipped a carafe near his "I Pray for My Pastor" coffee cup.

"I've had enough, Loren. Thank you." He placed his phone on privacy and joined the associates to banter money between departments. Sydney's senior portrait stared up at him from his credenza next to her ballet photograph, her kindergarten Polaroid, and the candid snapshot of her laughing in her daddy's arms at the Washington Zoo. Wade joined the men in body while his heart made a trench around the past.

AFTER ALLIE COMPLAINED about the rain for the third time, Sydney led them into the library. Her big fabric bag stuffed with clothes drew the librarian's eye. A high school friend once taught her how to move with an arrogant sort of surety whenever the movie theater usher stared suspiciously at their purses full of candy. "Children's books, please," said Sydney. She approached the desk with that borrowed air.

"Through this hall and to the right. You'll see the signs."

"I like the library," said Trevor. "In Florida last summer, Grammy took us every Saturday."

"She used to take me too," said Sydney.

Trevor read to Allie, both of them cradled in a beanbag chair. He invented the story dependent upon the illustrations. Sydney borrowed a phone book from the front desk. With a pencil and paper from the computer center, she copied down the motels with cheaper-looking advertisements.

Faded prints of significant men had hung on the wall for so long the stringy filaments of dust and webs had made a home. A clutter of newspapers, *Time* magazines, and discarded adhesive notes almost hid the student librarian behind the juveniles' counter. He was a lanky boy who snoozed on a stool only to startle awake whenever a child asked him to help find a book.

Trevor struck up a conversation with two other preschoolers. The foursome bantered about dragon stories and T-ball. The other mom glanced up from her novel and smiled at Sydney. Content in the scene before her, the mother fell back into her reading. Sydney fell back into the phone book. The library closed at five. She watched the minutes escape. With one finger, she picked out a motel with cheap rates and wrote down the address.

Trevor wanted to check out books. She read to him from two and then explained that library books would add to their load.

A jagged streak of lightning flashed outside. Allie cringed.

"We'll stay in here for as long as we can," said Sydney. She checked the clock again. Only two hours until five.

SYDNEY PAID THE CABDRIVER. She couldn't just ride around New Orleans all evening with Trevor and Allie. Her cash dwindled. She used part of the twenty from the gold ring to buy the deli sandwiches. But tomorrow's sunrise would bring the need for breakfast. Trevor was beginning to question why they hadn't gone home. Sydney was wondering herself why she had brought them to this old motel with the garish neon sign buzzing like a wounded mosquito.

"It's getting late," said Trevor. "I want to go home, Mommy."

"We can't. No electricity." She told the truth. Waking up to no electricity was what had started the argument between Ray and her. He had sold her car months ago, saying how they had to cut back on expenses. Now the electric bill was unpaid. But she didn't know about it until it was too late. For that she felt responsible. Ray had insisted on taking care of the bills, handing her a little cash each week for groceries with the promise that when he got his "in" at Exxon their finances would rebound.

Sydney opened the glass door to the motel office. Allie lay crumpled against her shoulder, asleep, while Trevor held to her right leg. "Do you have a room?" she asked.

A sleepy attendant glanced up from computer solitaire. "How long you need it?"

"One night."

"All night?"

"Of course, all night."

"Hey, *cher,* a real customer." A thin woman who wore a too-small cotton dress rested on an orange vinyl sofa. She lit a cigarette and then rested her colorless arm atop the sofa back.

"Shut up, Corette!" The motel clerk never made eye contact with Sydney. "You want me to turn the phone on, miss?"

"Of course. How much is that?"

"Twenty-five bucks held against the phone bill. The rest is refunded."

"If you're lucky," said Corette.

"Corette, you got other things to be done, now off wit' you."

"Me, I ain't got nothing to do 'cept watch the news. Ain't nothing going on around here till after eight."

"I think that I should shop around, maybe think about this," said Sydney.

"You don't want the room?" the clerk asked.

"No. That is, I want to check out the other motels."

"You want to burn cab fare, you go on. You want the cheapest room on the west side, you come to the right place. It's Wednesday night. You come back later, maybe I'll be too full to help you out."

24

"How much is the room?"

"Twenty-nine dollars, ninety-five cents plus phone fee, and I already told you what that costs."

"How many beds?"

"One full, and I'll throw in the cot for the boy. That girl baby, she can sleep wit' you?"

"I'll take it. But is it safe here?"

"You running from the law?"

"I mean safe for me, for my children."

"*Chère,* sure you safe here wit' ol' Pierre. Anybody mess wit' you, you just open your door and give me a yell. I'll throw out any trouble comes your way, eh."

Sydney paid him for the room and took the key.

"No phone, then?"

"No phone."

"Grandpa wouldn't like us staying here." Trevor tightened his grip around his mother's leg.

"It's for one night, Trevor. It's a bed and electricity."

"'Course electricity," said Pierre. "Kitchenette, color TV—we got it all here at Gaston's Budget Palace. You come by after six in the morning, and Mamie, she'll have some cereal set out for your kids and you."

"Since when you start continental breakfast, Pierre?" Corette asked.

"Always, when a customer stays the whole night. Now I axed you to leave, Corette."

Corette pretended to fidget with her strands of bleached hair that, from the neon glaring through the plate glass, had a pink cast.

"We'll take the cereal, thank you." After Sydney walked the

children back out into the wet night, she could see Pierre and Corette fighting; Pierre wagged his finger while Corette pointed with her cigarette. "Mommy's sorry, Trevor. I'll get a job tomorrow. Don't worry, honey."

"Is Daddy still mad at us?" Trevor asked.

"Let's hurry. The sun's almost down. I don't want to be out in this parking lot after dark."

"Can we call Grandpa again? Tell him to come get us, Mommy. He'll come. Grammy will tell him to come."

"I can't afford the phone, Trevor."

"You could call him on the pay phone and he'll pay for it."

"Trevor, that's enough! I can take care of us. Grandpa will just, well, he might get mad at us too. I shouldn't have called him today. We'll have to do this on our own."

"If you tell him, maybe he'll pray and—"

"Let's don't talk anymore until we get inside, Trevor. Mommy's tired. Let's get cleaned up and I'll read to you."

Sydney slid the old key into the door and, after dislodging the door from the thrice-painted frame, coaxed Trevor inside. She leaned against the door as the sun dissolved from the Louisiana sky. She looked up and down the walk until she was sure she wasn't being followed, then locked herself inside the stale room.

"I THINK WE OUGHT TO FLY to Louisiana, Wade." Isabella paced in front of the white provincial desk where she had once taught Sydney math.

"And go where, Izz? Sydney hasn't called us back. She's

patched things up with Ray and they're holed up in a Burger King somewhere, recounting their years of marital bliss."

"Ray doesn't answer the phone when I call."

"That's because he always makes Sydney answer it, makes her deal with the bill collectors."

"Sydney doesn't answer; Ray doesn't answer. We're to presume from their absence that they've taken a second honeymoon?"

"Husbands and wives quarrel, Isabella. I've counseled more than a few couples. Trust me on this one—it will blow over."

"You don't know everything about Ray, Wade."

"I just heard the doorbell. You want me to get it?"

"It's the pizza deliveryman. I hope you have some cash on you."

"That distinct bouquet from the kitchen is not dinner?"

"It's for the meals ministry. The Pendersnooks had their baby. I haven't had a chance to cook for us tonight, not and worry about Sydney too."

"So Mrs. Pendersnooks is handed Isabella's savory delectables in a basket with a ribbon while I get Pizza Pony Express?"

"I cooked for *Mr.* Pendersnooks. His wife is still in the hospital."

"So, I should have myself admitted just to get a decent meal."

"That would be a sight. Wade Jenkins having a baby." Isabella stood with her arms crossed, her gaze purposefully looking away from Wade.

He followed her gaze to Sydney's photo on the piano. "What don't I know?"

"About Mr. Pendersnooks?"

"About Ray. You said that I don't know everything about Ray."

"He's not a good husband."

"That's news?"

"In the worst sense, Wade."

"You're not telling me everything."

"I've tried, but you lose your temper about Sydney so much."

"I don't lose my temper. You exaggerate—just like Sydney."

"That's why she can't talk to you."

"She can't talk to me? It's easy—she dials the number. I answer. We talk."

"When you're in this frame of mind, Wade, we just don't communicate."

"Have you been listening to Dobson again?"

"What does Dr. Dobson have to do with our problems?"

"Every time you listen to that broadcast, you're mad at me when I come home."

"See how you evade the subject, Wade?"

"I'll go pay the Pony Express driver before he electrocutes himself on the doorbell."

"I'll fix us two iced teas."

"Maybe Vince Pendersnook needs a visit from the pastor tonight. I'll take him the basket, keep him company." Wade opened the door and pulled out his wallet.

"No need. Evelyn Gordon is picking up the food basket. I'm all finished with my obligation. I wonder where she is? She's always so prompt."

"Here's two bucks extra and keep the change." Wade stood with the hot cardboard box warming his hands. "Evelyn just pulled into the driveway." He waved and said, "Quick, Isabella, filch me a drumstick!"

"It isn't fried chicken. I made potpies."

"Plural?"

"Edie Pendersnook had a cesarean. She'll be in the hospital for days. He'll need the extra." She let out a sigh. "If you don't want pizza—"

"I didn't say I don't want pizza. Hello, Evelyn."

"Pastor, greetings. Is this the food for Mr. Pendersnook?" Evelyn took the pizza box from his hands.

"I hope he enjoys it, Evelyn. Give him my best." Wade tried to close the door.

"Evelyn!" Isabella breezed by Wade. "Please come in." She escorted Evelyn past Wade. He felt the Pizza Pony Express box slide back into his fingers. Isabella's eyes paled when she was angered. All of the warmth, he imagined, went south and settled in her feet by sheer force of her will. Her polar look could melt lava rocks.

"That pizza wasn't for Mr. Pendersnook?" Wade asked. "I misunderstood. My apologies, Evelyn." He dropped the pizza box onto Isabella's French provincial table next to her beaded memories box, which displayed a photo in the lid. Sydney stared up at him from the snapshot. Her ten-year-old eyes were wide, as though she were asking a question that he somehow along the way had never answered.

He lifted the lid on the cardboard pizza box. The contents had a limp look. What some pizza places called New York style, he called floppy: a pathetic excuse for wet dough. Give him a nice thin, crispy southern dough—now that's Italian. The phone rang. Before he could say, "I'll get it," Isabella scooped up the receiver in the kitchen and cradled it between her jaw and shoulder while she checked the contents of the food basket. "Hello!" she said. "Sydney?"

"Thank you so much for sharing your dinner with the

Pendersnooks," Evelyn gushed. "Pastor, you and Isabella are by far the dearest pastoral family we've ever had. I'm in the choir and I so look forward to your Christmas narration. Are you coming to rehearsal tonight?"

Wade tried to listen to Isabella, to try and discern whether Sydney had called. He patted Evelyn's hand and then picked up the extension.

"Wade, is that you?" Isabella asked. "It's Sam Farris. He wants to ask you about the Christmas rehearsal."

Evelyn smiled at Wade.

"Pastor, are you there?" Sam Farris asked.

"I'm here."

"If you could just come tonight, we want to block out the scenes, and it will help the cast and choir, at least for this first rehearsal."

"Sam, thank you for thinking of me, but as I mentioned earlier . . ."

"Isabella, you're so fortunate to have such a gifted husband. Is there anything he can't do?" Evelyn propped up the basket of potpies on one hip.

Although Isabella smiled, she expressed only a trace of emotion from her eyes, a signal that she desired a private moment with her husband.

∽◯∾

A SIGN ABOVE the motel room lamp said TURN OFF LIGHTS WHEN YOU LEAVE THE ROOM. PUT CIGARETTE BUTTS IN ASHTRAY.

Sydney left the lamp on. Her stomach had roiled every night

with a new cauldron of jitters for the last six months. Ray's new friends sometimes stayed until dawn. Ray told her she had no reason to mistrust them, but she made Allie and Trevor sleep with her on those nights. Ray's depression turned into a different style of creature when his friends from the east side made their weekend appearance. Somehow she feared she had brought them all with her.

Allie nestled a doll while she lay with her lips pressed against the pillow. She nuzzled the pillow to fall asleep. Her lashes brushed the pillowcase like a gentle broom.

"Allie, you still awake?"

"No, Mommy."

"I've never seen that doll before."

"It's a new doll."

"I don't remember buying a new doll."

"It's Daddy's."

"You mean he gave it to you."

"No. Daddy's doll. I found it where he keeps his guns."

Sydney often warred with Ray over keeping guns under the bed. "You're not supposed to get in Daddy's box. Anyway, he keeps it locked."

"But it was open. I found this dolly in the gun box."

"Let me hold the dolly," said Sydney. She tried to slide it out of Allie's hands.

"No, he bought it for me. He wouldn't buy anybody but me a doll."

"I'll give it right back. Just let me see it."

The head wobbled when Allie held it out to her. The faded satin dress had missing snaps in the back. "It's a cloth doll. Really

31

old. Someone's tried to repair it. When I get a needle and thread, I'll resew it if you really like it. I wonder why Ray never told me about it?"

"He was saving her for me. But I already found her. Her name is Grammy 'cause she's old."

"Here, you go to sleep. It's really late."

Allie held the doll next to her. Her eyelids batted shut. The doll stared wide eyed from painted-on eyes.

The doll smelled dirty to Sydney. When Allie fell asleep, she would put it away for her until she could figure out a way to clean it or just throw it out. "Good night, Grammy," Sydney whispered. The night took over more swiftly than Sydney expected. Gaston's Budget Palace lacked streetlights and door lights. A blindfold fell across the place except for the lamp in room thirty-two and the headlights of the customers who had just started to arrive.

5

WADE FINISHED HIS ORANGE JUICE by the pool. Sleep had fled him the night before. After a brief appearance at the Christmas rehearsal, he dragged himself home and found Isabella awake. Both of them reshuffled the sheets so many times, he found the top sheet twisted around his ankles by morning.

Sunrise came too early. The morning light always pierced through the shades in one small beam that hit him square between the eyes. He threw on his robe and slippers, took Isabella up on her offer of freshly squeezed juice, and read the paper out by the swimming pool. The pool had been Sydney's idea, although she and the kids had enjoyed it only for a brief week last summer.

Isabella had grown a hedge of bright pink rhododendron around the perimeter. Wade felt as though he sat in the middle of a bouquet every morning. He picked up the empty glass and met Isabella inside the breakfast nook. She followed him to the bedroom.

"I slept none, Wade, none at all last night. My eyes look like beets."

"If it will make you feel any better, Isabella, then try and call Sydney's apartment again," Wade said. He watched her open and close the venetian blinds, dust them again, and then raise them.

"You haven't called her yet, have you?"

"This tie doesn't match my shirt. Does it?"

"Maybe she's really home, but she is waiting to hear your voice, her own father's voice, and then she'll pick up the phone." She adjusted her shoulders in a way that reminded him of when she was twenty-one, a frail-boned beauty who thought the ministry was a romantic adventure.

"You stage these scenes in your head so much, Isabella, you begin to believe them. Maybe I won't wear a tie. Banks have casual Friday. I'll declare today is Casual Thursday. That would rumple the feathers of a few board members—my making a dress-code change. I'd especially like to see Hazzleby's face. I should do it."

"What if it's true and you never tried to call her, Wade?" They both wandered out into the hall.

"You call. If she's home, hand the phone to me. I'm changing shirts."

"Is it really Casual Thursday?"

"Call Sydney. I'll wait by the extension in the bedroom."

"What is the signal?"

He stood at the mouth of the hallway. "What signal, Isabella?"

"To let you know if Sydney answers the phone."

"How about 'Hello, Sydney!'"

"That's good, Wade. I'll say it nice and loud."

"I'll go change my shirt." Wade pulled his silk necktie away from the collar.

"Hello, Sydney?"

He froze.

"That was a rehearsal."

He stared at her until his pupils lost their glow.

"I'm dialing. Hurry." She flailed her hand in a shooing motion.

Isabella had burned cherry-scented candles during her morning devotion. It made their bedroom smell like Tootsie Pops. He felt like a stranger in the bedroom. All of the furniture pieces he and Isabella had struggled to purchase just to take up the yawning spaces of the trailer they lived in during Bible college had one by one disappeared like specters. All of the old bedroom furniture had been progressively replaced with contemporary woods and pale Floridian colors sated with peach and turquoise fabrics. Isabella wanted few reminders of their past financial struggles. Only the kids' school pictures remained in clustered arrangements on one long wall, each one framed in discount store casings, dated by eighties' haircuts; Isabella had always made certain their hairstyles meshed with the decade. Sydney had tried to buy all those old school portraits from her mother just so she could burn them. Isabella won out. For once.

Wade put away the necktie. He pulled out a polo shirt, a yellow one with a swordfish crest. It was too casual, he decided. More like a car salesman. Isabella hated that shirt. Then he pulled out a chambray shirt. Better, he decided. He could carry a necktie in his coat pocket and put it on later if the need arose for a tie.

A gecko crawled across the window, tongue darting as though in disapproval. *Sigh*. Even the lizards criticized him.

He put the chambray back in the closet, put the pale blue dress shirt back on, tied his tie, buttoned his coat, and decided to send out a note the next week about Casual Thursday. Or maybe he should institute it on Fridays, like the banks did. Too much change might cause an overload in the criticism box.

He had forgotten to listen for Isabella's signal. He could hear her muttering. With his ear to the door, he could scarcely make out her words. But her voice needled the air, pinpricks followed by quiet sighs. Her distress ebbed toward him and made him sigh again. He pulled off his coat and lifted the telephone receiver to his ear. The voice on the other end made him feel sour. It was Sydney's husband, Ray. If Wade tried to hang up now, Isabella would hear the click. He laid the receiver on its side and crept out into the hallway.

Isabella's forehead was pinched and taut. She covered the receiver with one hand. "It's Ray," she whispered. "He sounds . . . ruffled."

Wade stared at her, pursed his lips, and allowed his shoulders to drop and his brows to lift, a silent question.

"Ruffled. Like he just woke up." She whispered again.

"Just tell him you want to talk to Sydney. Don't give him time to think."

"No, you tell him. In your . . . 'man' way."

"I forgot my coat. I'll be right back. Go ahead and ask him." He could hear her voice all the way into the bedroom, breathy and weak. She was asking for Sydney, every word grasping, hopeful the reply would unearth a little honesty from an otherwise dishonest man. Guilt crept in. Wade shouldn't have handed Isabella the dirty work. The receiver still lay on its side. He lifted it to his ear and listened.

Ray Oliver was a lousy liar. He was telling Isabella that Sydney and the kids had gone to stay with a friend in Shreveport. But Wade knew that Sydney's only friend in Shreveport had moved away six months ago. Isabella must have forgotten.

"Ray, this is Wade. I want to know where my daughter and grandkids are."

Isabella's relief bubbled out between breaths. "Ray says Sydney's taken the kids to Shreveport, Wade," Isabella answered for him. "What is that girl's name? Do we have her number, Wade?"

"Whitney," Wade said. "She moved from Shreveport six months ago, Ray. I want to know why Sydney called my office crying and then never called us back."

"I'll hang up and let you men talk."

Wade heard Isabella's nervous click on the other phone.

"If the two of you got along, Wade, she might call you more often." Ray coughed.

"Fine. If you don't answer my questions, maybe you'll talk to the police!"

"If Sydney lied to me about her Shreveport friend, is it my fault? You know how emotional she gets at the slightest problem. One little thing goes wrong, and off she goes on one of her tangents."

"Isabella has been calling night and day since Monday. She left messages. It isn't like Sydney not to call her mother back. I want you to think, Ray. Has she been gone since Monday? Tuesday?"

"Tuesday, I think. She calls me every night. But I guess she lied about Shreveport."

"Sydney's not a liar." Wade clenched the phone. "Her car was having brake problems. Is there a chance she's had an accident? Have you tried to call the authorities yourself?"

"She sounds okay on the phone. And her brakes are fixed. I fixed them myself. Look, I have to go to work. If I'm late, I lose my job."

"One more question—"

The line went dead.

✑

SYDNEY LAY CURLED between Trevor and Allie, her eyes closed. She evoked memories of the sounds outside the bedroom window of her folks' Florida home: her mother humming a tune to God while she pruned the roses that bloomed all winter; the neighbor's Shih Tzu yapping to the cadence of the underground sprinklers. All of life so completely ordinary, it had slipped her mind to remember to love it.

The parking lot at Pierre Gaston's Budget Palace was quiet in the early hours with most of the customers either gone or passed out drunk, sleeping off the effects of the night's activities. Sydney listened to the roar of the semi trucks that blared noisy horns and wheeled around the commuters who traversed the eternal stretch of sooty Airline Highway.

If she were back in her apartment right now, neighbor Arlen Guitreau would be out on his five-by-five cracked concrete landing, salting down the chicken and sausage in his simmering pot for jambalaya. Neighborhood children would be collecting at the door to ask Trevor and Allie to come play, all of them dressed in last year's ragged garments so they could save their better things for school.

Ray would have no awareness of any of it. He would sleep as

the phone rang, commencing the ambush of the coming weekend's bill collectors. By Sunday night, his agitation would play out through two empty six-packs and a rising obsession that Sydney had instigated the conflicts between them. Ray's friends always disappeared whenever they fought. Sunday night's dread would fuel Monday's tirade.

Allie sneezed.

"Time to wake up," said Sydney.

"No, let us sleep." Trevor pulled the sheet over his head.

Allie slept with her mouth open.

Soft footsteps were heard outside on the walk. Then came the knock. Wary of Pierre's primal mix of customers, Sydney hesitated.

Another knock.

"Somebody's here," said Trevor. "Maybe Grandpa came."

Sydney pulled back the blinds. "It's Corette." She turned the dead bolt and then waved her in.

"I had me this idea," Corette said and flicked her cigarette outside the door. "Oh, that baby girl's sleeping. How doll-like she looks with her dark curls. Me, I have to use Miss Clairol to get a color that dark. I finally went blonde. You like my hair?" It still looked pink, even by day.

"What idea, Corette?"

"I talked to Pierre. He been needing a good cleaning woman. You been needing money, true? So you clean rooms for him and you get your roof free plus breakfast for the little ones."

"I can't stay here, Corette."

"Don't get all uppity, girl. You need money. Pierre, he can pay you cash at the end of every day. Just 'til you get back on your feet."

"I'm in a bad situation, Corette. It's bad enough I stayed here one night. I can't let anyone know I'm here with Trevor and Allie. I'm a bad mother."

"Who goin' to know? Me, I tell no one. I keep my mouth shut."

"Allie, time to wake up. Let's go eat cereal," said Sydney.

"He'll pay you six an hour and he's got a lot to clean, especially on the weekends."

"I hear thunder again." Sydney glanced through the dingy glass. The sky gathered the billows into iron gray clusters to spit rain upon the just aroused Big Easy. Winter never turned cold enough for heavy woolens or warm enough for summer outfits. She never knew exactly how to dress the kids. Whatever she layered them with in the morning was peeled off by midday. "I wish I had my car." The headlights of the seven o'clock traffic turned the streets into murky mirrors.

"I'm ready for cereal." Allie stood with one sock on and a sweater pulled over her nightgown. She lisped her words but said them with such a saccharine vigor that she always made strangers chuckle. Corette laughed.

"Trevor, please find a shirt for your sister. I'll find her shoes." The smell of tobacco draped the air where Corette stood. But her company put Sydney at ease, made her feel not so alone.

"I'm sorry if I bothered you," Corette said. "You good people don't need the likes of me hanging around." She stepped toward the door, her bowed silhouette so frail in appearance, a good wind might send her tumbling.

"You're not bothering me." Sydney pulled Allie's sneaker over the red sock she had donned. "I'm sure you don't like to get up so early just to find jobs for nervous women."

"I don't know how a girl like you ended up here on dis side of town. You got your own story. I'll bet it's a good one."

"I made a mistake. I never should have left school."

"You go to school here, in town?"

"LSU. I once went. I met someone who worked in the school commons. He told me everything I wanted to hear, anything to make me believe we had the same ambitions."

"That would be all men."

"I don't know, Corette. I've only really known one besides my dad."

"Your daddy, he must be dead or you would have called him by now, I'll bet."

Sydney combed Allie's hair into ringlets.

"I won't axe you no more."

"How did you meet Pierre?"

"Ol' Pierre. I been on my own since I was sixteen. I never had no sense when it come to books or math. Pierre found me near dead, gave me a room. I split my income with him."

"He has more girls than just you?"

"Three more. Pierre don't beat his girls. He's good to us."

"Still. He makes you believe you can't climb any higher, that you can't make it on your own."

"If he say that, he be right. I never met a woman so bright as you, though. You just need a little foot up and then you'll be sailing out of here. You got culture. Women with culture, they don't need any man telling them what to do. They just go do for themselves."

"You think?"

"I know. I'll tell Pierre you got better things to do than clean his smelly old motel."

"Wait, Corette." Sydney met her at the door. "You made me a decent offer. I should have the decency to take you up on it. Just for a few days."

"Just a few days, chère. I know you won't want to be around here a long time. I'll tell Pierre, just a few days, then."

"Are we going to live here?" Trevor asked.

"No, just until I can find a real job." Sydney pulled Allie's shirt over her head. "And a car."

Allie cheered. She liked the motel with free cereal and sociable neighbors.

6

WADE LIKED IT when Isabella sang. Out of habit, she always hummed around the kitchen. But when she sat next to him in the car, her entire bearing echoed the bohemian attitude of a Florida blue-sky day. Her shoulders swayed, her toes tapped, and she tossed little oblique glances at Wade, her invitation for him to join her.

He turned the car right on Park Boulevard and then left on Sixty-sixth to head toward the large St. Petersburg mall, Tyrone Square—the last place at which he wanted to waste a personal day's worth of precious time. But Isabella had awoken in a strange sort of Christmas shopping frenzy.

She bore down on the words to "Ain't No Mountain High Enough." She thought it was a gospel song, just like she thought "Stairway to Heaven" should be sung in a Billy Graham crusade.

"You're in a good mood. I'm glad."

She ignored him and began to fumble through her handbag.

"Or you've slipped off the hills of insanity. I knew that would happen."

"Wade, I've known for a long time that Sydney didn't belong with that man no more than she belongs in New Orleans. Once you go to New Orleans to fetch her, she'll come home. I believe she's finally had her fill of him. I'll watch the kids for her while she gets back on her feet, you know, finishes school. She has her pick of schools. I'll bet with her transcript, she can get into Eckerd."

"You have it all worked out then?"

"I do."

"I'm going to New Orleans?"

"Of course. Didn't we discuss your going to New Orleans?"

"No, we didn't."

"Last night?"

"I was at the church for the Christmas rehearsal. You were asleep when I came home."

"I could have sworn we talked about it. You will go, won't you?"

"And do what? Stand in the middle of New Orleans and shout until Sydney comes and jumps in my arms?"

"You have to think like Sydney thinks. Strategy, Wade. But you have to get there as soon as possible before that man finds her first and manipulates her again. Or worse."

"Don't you want them to stay married?"

"And why? So that evil Ray can destroy what's left of her spirit? She needs to come home and start all over."

"And live with us?"

"Of course, live with us. She can work in the church again," help out around the house. Just like before she ran off to that LSU and met Ray."

"She's not the same Sydney, Isabella. Sydney's a woman. She won't want to allow you to smooth out all the rough places for her, to doctor her wounds. Besides, Sydney didn't like volunteering at the church. She hated it, hated standing in front of a group of people."

"Sydney's still a girl. Just confused is all. And I'm still her mother. I know I can help if we can just get her back home."

"If I so much as offer a suggestion to her, she hangs up on me. You think she's going to get in the car with me and let me tell her how to fix all of her problems?"

"You shouldn't take the car. We haven't much time. I'll book the flights—one for you round-trip, and one-way for Sydney and the kids."

"Listen to yourself, Izz. You keep factoring Sydney out of the decision-making equation. First let's try and communicate with her on the phone, see how she's feeling right now. We don't know if she's had enough of Ray or is just trying to teach him a lesson."

"Ray's abusive, Wade. I've been trying to tell you that."

"In what way, and how do you know?"

"I hate to say this. . . . I know you might want to kill him, and you know how your temper can flare. Sydney thinks you'll take it out on her, make her feel like an idiot. But I just don't think I can keep mum about all of this."

"Out with it."

"He sold her car. And I hate to say this, but he's started drinking."

"Ray Oliver sold Sydney's car? The one we bought her for her high school graduation?"

"For being valedictorian, yes. It's gone. And she's been crying a lot, but she won't come out with everything. I think he hits her."

"I'll kill him."

"See, I knew you would."

"Just how long were you going to wait to tell me all of this?" He glanced at a pancake house, then focused ahead on the coming intersection.

"Sydney made me swear not to tell you. I think she feels ashamed."

"And well she should. I told her not to marry that mangy sneak. Then he off and moves her into some who-knows-what kind of dump. Don't look at me like that. She must live in a rat hole of a place, or why else would she put us off when we try to come and see them?"

"I imagine it's not much better than the place where we lived on the Bible school campus." Isabella made a right jab with her index finger when the light turned green. "Turn here."

"That was different. We were making something of ourselves, Izz. If Ray Oliver were in school while Sydney worked, well, it would at least be something to hope for. He's ambitionless."

"*Ambitionless.* Is that a word?"

"It's an apt description, and I'd venture to say he filled her head with all sorts of fabrications just to get her to say she'd marry him. I warned her about her romantic notions."

"Sydney was surely in love with love."

"And now she's hiding out in some who-knows-what sort of place in New Orleans—without a car! And what did Ray do with the money? Fixed her brakes, my eye!"

"Look at that parking lot, will you?"

Wade glanced across the intersection of Tyrone and Sixty-sixth. Glittering streamers and flags swayed from the parking lot lights. Not one parking space was unoccupied. He heaved a breath. "I can't believe you can shop, Isabella. Aren't you feeling all anxious like usual when you're worried about Sydney?"

"When you bring them home, I want to have the whole house smelling and ringing of Christmas—not a Florida Christmas, but a genuine mountain Christmas like we used to have in Tennessee. When Trevor and Allie see my tree and all Grammy's presents waiting for them, won't they be glad to be out of New Orleans?"

"Now who's manipulating?"

"It's not manipulation, Wade. It's a wake-up call, like when the prodigal's father had the big party waiting for his son. We'll be saying through our actions, 'Don't ever do anything like that again,' only with gifts and parties and all the things that remind Sydney of where she belongs."

"I can't find a parking place. It's nutso around here!"

"Park in the back row. The mall has golf carts this year. Let's hurry. I'm hungry."

Wade parked. He looked out across the overcrowded parking lot while a golf-cart driver shuttled them toward the food court entrance and bounced the two of them over several speed bumps. Isabella rattled off her to-buy list. Transplanted palm trees lilted over the asphalt, staked into the potting beds, sort of trapped in appearance, lost, nodding to one another about sandy coves.

"I wonder if Sydney has gotten back down to a size six petite. When she went on that ice-cream binge with her second pregnancy, it liked to have ruined her waistline. But she looks small again in that portrait she sent of the kids and herself. Wonder why Ray didn't sit with them for that picture?"

"I wonder. Driver, we can get off here. I'd like to walk off what I'm about to eat." Wade helped Isabella from the cart and handed the man two dollars.

"I should get them all something to wear. They won't have as much space here in our two extra bedrooms for too many knick-knacks. Oh, but I have to buy those sweet things a few toys. But aren't you glad, Wade, that we went ahead and bought the four-bedroom like I wanted?"

"After you." He opened the plate-glass door and followed her into the food court.

"I know you think that I haven't noticed that you aren't answering me. But I do notice things like that, and how you think that I don't have a cognizant thought in my head."

"Salad bar or burger?"

"Things like that irk me, Wade. How you have a completely different conversation than I'm having, that is what really boils my pot!"

"Are you saying you want to fight, Isabella? I have to battle with the improvements committee on Monday morning, languish over debt reduction at the year-end meeting Monday afternoon, sleep through the church board meeting on Tuesday and the staff meeting on Wednesday. Shall I pencil you in for an argument on Friday?"

"I don't want to fight. I just want an answer."

"Then ask me the question. Clue me in, Isabella."

"What have we been talking about the last half hour, for crying out loud?"

"Our stubborn daughter and her obnoxious husband. If you asked me a question, it escaped me. I'm sorry. Just ask it again. I'm really listening this time."

"Are you going to fly to New Orleans and bring back Sydney and the kids?"

∽⌒∾

BOTH OF THE CHILDREN watched cartoons from room to room while Sydney changed the bed linens. Allie dug the cloth rag doll out of Sydney's suitcase. She would not part with it no matter how much Sydney told her it reminded her of dirty socks.

"Trevor, not so loud with the TV."

Allie stacked clean ashtrays on the thin carpet. She stacked them into a sort of glass tower and called it her fish house.

"Let's don't get too noisy, kids. Corette says some of these people are still asleep." The sleepers were actually some of the women who worked for Gaston. But she did not want to pique Trevor's inquisitive imagination. "Give me two more minutes, and then we'll stop to have some lunch," said Sydney.

"I want a burger," said Trevor.

"More like a cheese sandwich," said Sydney. "We'll work toward burgers next week."

"This place is old." Trevor held out the remote and surfed through three fuzzy channels until he found a good one. "They don't even have Cartoon Network."

"Neither do we," said Sydney.

"Motels are supposed to have everything." Trevor settled on a public broadcasting channel.

Sydney corner-tucked the drab off-white sheet near the foot-board. The polyester bedspread weighed only a few ounces. She had spotted this same coverlet on a bargain shelf at a grocery store once. Some marketing genius had suspended the row of bedspreads above the orange juice cases. Pierre Gaston must have made a deal with the grocery store.

Garish paisley prints decorated each motel room: swirls of pink and paisley eyes that swirled into green centers. Some of the carpets were pink, faded like stuffed animals left out in the sun; around the beds the pink carpet appeared almost bleached, a diluted champagne color that turned rose and then darkened at the bright pink edges near the baseboards. Gaston had installed teal carpet in other rooms—the rooms he called his Business Package. Those quarters came with continental breakfast, a clock radio, and in-room movies. Sydney noticed at least one BMW parked in front of a door to a Business Package.

She and Allie gathered the ashtrays back onto her maid's cart. "You need your nap. I don't know how to make beds and give you your nap all at once."

"I'll watch her," said Trevor.

"You need a nap too. I'll just have to finish the rest of the rooms later. Gaston doesn't need them until late anyway."

"People come here late at night, but they don't spend the night." Trevor reached for the cart handle.

"Not only did I buy cheese and bread, but we have apples and juice too." Sydney attempted to change the subject.

"Does it cost a lot?" said Trevor.

"What? Apples?"

"No. To stay here if you don't sleep?"

Sydney steered them down the walk and up to their room. She wondered about things like a little boy's memory and how she could tell him later this place was nothing more than a bad dream. Ray always said that lies could help people reach for things that made them forget they lived in misery. She could hear him say it just like that, standing there with his sleeves rolled up to the elbows, bent over the L-shape of the kitchen counter as he doled out his philosophies. She felt like a carbon Ray as she scrounged through her purse, desperate for pocket change.

"Trevor, never forget that we came to this place," said Sydney.

"Why, Mommy?"

"Because we want to remember what it feels like to want something better."

"Like a hamburger."

"Sure. And then we move up from there."

ISABELLA HAD NITPICKED most of the time while Wade picked at his cheeseburger, so much so that he finally abandoned the eating of it, ushered her off to shopping land, and found an ice-cream shop with a nearby bench. He sat next to a fiftyish-looking man who was clad in a plaid shirt and toted a backpack.

"Wife off shopping?" the man said.

Wade nodded, spooned a large mound of chocolate macadamia-nut ice cream into his mouth, and watched Isabella disappear into the swarm.

"I always tell her, 'As long as I can find a bench and an ice-cream shop, I'll drive you.' Name's Bob." He held out his hand to Wade.

Wade shook it. "Must be a thousand people here in this place."

"Or more. I can always tell when Eliza's in that shopping

mood. Lovey—I like to call her that—wakes up with a strange glimmer in her eyes, her pupils small as pinheads."

Wade chuckled. "I'm Wade." He dispensed with the "pastor" title, more interested in male dialogue. "Now that we have grand-kids, Isabella's even more relentless about Christmas shopping."

"You don't look old enough."

Wade started to pull out the photos but thought how Florid-ian-retiree he looked doing it. "Trevor and Allie. They look just like their mother." And then, as though only he could hear, "Thankfully."

"Don't guess I'll have grandkids."

"Sure you will. They all get married sooner or later."

Bob held up a photo so fast, Wade figured it must have been in his jacket pocket. "My son, Marcus."

"Nice-looking fellow. Athletic. He in college?"

"He was."

A family from Clearwater Freewill stopped all at once and waved at Wade while one of the children said meekly, "Hi, Pastor."

"You're a pastor?" Bob said.

Wade took another lick of ice cream and waved until the last child disappeared into a jewelry store. "Clearwater Freewill Taber-nacle."

"Say, that's a nice big church."

"Where does Marcus live?"

"He attended Florida State almost two years ago. Had him a nice apartment, met a girl. Pretty girl."

Wade held the cone between two hands and glanced at Bob. Bob's voice had lowered two decibels since he had started talking about Marcus.

"Marcus and I had been on the outs for a while. He had taken off for a year, gone off to Europe, toured on a bike with some of his buddies with just a few things in a backpack and worked here and yon. Dreamers, I called them. Said he wanted to travel. I was against it. Thought he ought to graduate college first. But he wouldn't have any of my advice."

"They never do."

"Took lots of pictures, he did, and met a girl in Brussels."

"European?"

"No. I wondered why he had to travel all the way to Brussels just to meet a girl from Oklahoma. But that was Marcus for you. He wrote his mother and myself a letter. Said he hoped things could be better between us when he got back. His mother, of course, was all for that. But I told her to give him some time to think about how he had gotten so mad at me that day he left. I wanted a full-fledged apology, I guess."

"They never do that."

"He got back home late, they say, to pack up at his apartment. He and that girl, Marcie, were going to marry and find their own place. I don't know if he was coming to see us the next day or not."

The ice cream had lost its flavor. Wade tucked the remaining cone into a paper bag. "You don't have to tell me if you don't want."

"Some lady's Christmas tree caught fire, or her Christmas lights went bad, something like that. Anyhow, Marcus had to play the hero. Ran out into the street with his backpack full of photos, handed it to a neighbor, then ran back into the apartment building to save that lady's four kids."

"I'm sorry."

"I met Marcie at Marcus's funeral. She didn't know what to say to me. Just handed me this backpack full of photos. For a long time, I kept them in the attic. Too painful. I take them out now from time to time. Here, let me show you." Bob opened the backpack. "Here he is with a group of students from Brussels. Don't they all look like they're looking at him, like, well, as though he's the leader of the pack? I keep trying to figure out all the things I didn't know about my boy just by studying these photos. I don't know what would make him want to fly halfway around the world just to ride a bike, sleep under the stars, and meet a girl who shared the same dreamy ambitions. I don't know what sent him into that burning building."

Wade handed the photo back to Bob. "He looks as though his last months were happy ones."

"He must have had a kind heart, don't you think? Surely he knew I loved him. You think?" A mist settled in his eyes, rimmed his bottom lashes.

Wade laid his hand atop Bob's. "I'm sure he knew, Bob. You can remember Marcus as a hero."

"I see the missus coming with her packages. Guess I've talked your ear off, Pastor."

"Please, just Wade. I'm glad I met you, Bob."

"Wade. I like that. I'll bet your church folks are really fond of you." Bob adjusted the backpack and waved at a heavyset woman with a jovial face. "Coming, Lovey. Bye, Wade."

Wade lifted his hand and waved it back and forth until Bob walked away with his wife.

Five hired Dickens-styled carolers paused near the food court to sing, dressed in velvet and taffeta costumes. Their harmony was precise and resonated with the lyrics from "Silent Night." The youngest, a small dark-haired girl, stood front and center dressed more like a Dickens's ragpicker. She clutched a bag labeled with the name of a charity. She passed it around to the shoppers, who stopped to watch. Just beyond them, the mall's Santa gathered two small children on his knee, a boy and a girl about the age of Trevor and Allie.

Wade mulled over Bob's story. He felt as though he had had a visit from a Christmas ghost.

"I wanted a full-fledged apology, I guess. Said he hoped things could be better between us when he got back. His mother, of course, was all for that."

Wade could picture Trevor's and Allie's faces as they waited in a harsh place. He felt as though he could read Sydney's fear. Isabella had sensed it somehow—he had not tried hard enough to reach them this week. His chest felt tight. He coughed but could not get enough air. Pressing his hand against his chest and throat, he massaged but could not rub away the pain around his heart. The crowd around him seemed to sway and then encircle him. The voices were distorted. A woman shouted. Faces gathered above, asking him questions he could not answer. He had to find Sydney. He had to get up off this bench. His limbs had no feeling, and he felt stretched out and splayed. ANOTHER RELIC KEELS OVER IN FLORIDA, the headlines would read.

"Call 911!" a youth yelled.

He tried to wave them away, to tell them he was fine, that he only needed to find his daughter and grandkids and bring them home, safe and sound. But the colors around him swirled into a gray vortex as the air roared things he could not understand, until the last thing he saw was the worried, gentle face of Isabella. *Please, God, don't let me die in a mall.* After that, he saw only darkness.

7

"PANIC ATTACK? That sounds like something a woman would have." Wade lay stretched out on his recliner while Isabella fed him aspirin and cola.

"Wade, I'm a woman. I've never had a panic attack."

"You have them all the time, Isabella. You panicked at least twice this week."

"Worry attacks and panic attacks are not the same thing."

"I think that doctor is whacked. Maybe I should see another doctor."

"Depends on how you feel right now."

"I feel fine. I don't want any more of your aspirin, Isabella. Just give me the Coke, is all."

"You must have been as worried about Sydney as I am. What

happened before your 'panic attack'? For instance, what was going
on when you first started, well, swirling, as you said?"

"Not 'swirling,' and don't say 'panic attack' at church or to
any of the ladies at those meetings you attend. I don't need gossip
spreading around that the pastor is having some sort of, well, spells."

"Spells. You say that like my Aunt Rhoda has 'spells.' People
have panic attacks, Wade. It's normal these days. I read about it in
Ladies' Home Journal."

"See, that's just the kind of talk I don't need. Please just do
what I say, Isabella. Keep this between us."

"Oh, anyway, I think it's too late, Wade. You know the
Johnsons were at the mall. Bev Johnson's called twice already and
put you on the phone prayer chain."

"Tell me you're kidding me."

"I'm not."

"By the time this makes the rounds, they'll have me strung out
at the Betty Ford Center."

"You still didn't answer my question—what were you thinking about when all this started?"

"I don't remember." The napkin that was wrapped around the
glass of cola developed a drip. He peeled it from the glass and
dropped it onto the *St. Petersburg Times*. "I sat next to some guy
who had lost a son. It just made me think about Sydney, how we
don't know how much time we have with each other. I had this sort
of choking feeling. I couldn't breathe. Honestly, I thought it was a
heart attack."

"I shouldn't have pushed you to go and find them. It's my
fault, I guess. Imagine, you running around who knows where.
You were right. I was wrong."

"No, you were right, Izz. As a matter of fact, I feel as though I can't get to Louisiana fast enough."

"Oh, Wade, you're not going? Shouldn't you be in bed or something?"

"I've made up my mind, Isabella. Somehow, I'm bringing them back home—if Sydney doesn't hate me too much."

"Sydney doesn't hate you. She just gets put out, like her father."

"I'm going to go into the office right now and tie up loose ends. I'll get two of the associates to take a service each for me Sunday."

"Who, Sam Farris?"

"He's got all the choir to contend with. Maybe Loren Matthews."

"The youth group would like that."

"He needs the practice anyway. Can't stay a youth pastor forever. And I should probably call Grace Huddleston. She wanted to move up the date for her daughter's wedding, but they are just going to have to wait. I don't have the time, and besides, I don't feel comfortable marrying two young kids all in a rush like Suzie and Buzz."

"Don't let them talk you into doing something you don't believe is right. Suzie and Buzz can wait. Maybe I should just call Ray again and see if he's heard from Sydney. I should never have started all of this. What was I thinking?" She picked up the phone.

"Try and book me a flight tonight, say, after dinner."

Isabella sat with the receiver to her ear while the phone rang and rang, unanswered.

"ALLIE, you feel warm."

"My head hurts," said Allie. "And my throat, it's sore."

"Don't you get sick on me now." Sydney tucked the sheets around her.

"I'm sleepy."

"Your cheeks are red." With the back of her hand, she felt Allie's forehead and then her arm. "I'll see if I brought the thermometer." It didn't take long to rummage through their things and find the zipper sandwich bag full of a few medicines but no thermometer. "If I brought everything I needed, I guess we'd still be home, packing."

Allie stopped babbling. She slept while Sydney undressed her and covered her with the pale top sheet.

"Is she sick?" Trevor kicked off his shoes and climbed onto the full bed.

"Maybe. It could be a virus, or . . . I just don't know what's wrong." Sydney tossed out the paper plates from lunch and took their cups into the bathroom to wash them. Trevor fell asleep. She propped pillows against the headboard and sat vigil over Allie. The clock radio made an electronic tapping noise. It must have been left on all morning. Sydney adjusted the dial until the weatherman sounded clear but planted in the bottom of a well. The cold front might invade the south by Monday, with temperatures dipping to freezing even in the Florida panhandle.

Pierre Gaston passed by the window. He was paler in the daylight, a skinny man with thinning hair and a mustache he must have groomed himself. Everything about him was smarmy: the elongated stride with his hands always hidden in his pockets, those dark eyes that never stopped surveying the kingdom of Gaston. Under one lanky arm, he carried a moneybag that attached to his patent leather belt with a chain. He disappeared into a Business Package room, one that Corette had advised Sydney to make up later in the day.

Trevor left an open bag of marbles next to his socks on the floor. The thought of settling into the Budget Palace so irked Sydney that she would not put their things away into the two-drawer dresser. Trevor's token little boy things tended to get scattered several times a day. She picked up the marble bag and socks. A small photo twirled to the floor, a head shot of her father dressed in his best suit, an annoying gray wool with a cut that would be in style in the last decade or the next. Sydney remembered when her mother had insisted upon his sitting for this photo two months ago. Wade Jenkins had not posed for a photograph since his Bible school days. When he answered Trevor's first scrawled letter (penned phonetically and in five-year-old all-caps), he had tucked a wallet-size print of himself into the letter. On the back it said, "To the best boy in the world—Grandpa." Sydney jiggled the photograph back into the velvet bag and pulled the drawstring.

His face, the sight of it, brought little lectures back to her, sonnets of disapproval.

The bag of marbles clacked when she tossed it into the over-stuffed bag. Even from this distance, Wade Jenkins walked around inside her head: Wade and God talking about her, voicing disapproval, whispering and pondering how to woo her back to the fold. If Wade had never brought the church marching through the

Jenkins home, she could have lived with the God talk. Possibly she might have wanted some of it herself if she could have owned some of the room-for-error space, the place where people who can never seem to get it all just right are allowed to live. Maybe if, at her birth, her dad—Wade Jenkins the CEO or Wade Jenkins the housepainter—could have come in with the morning paper, looked over her crib, and announced that the Jenkins baby had been born and that had been the end of it, perhaps a little corner of her might have had room for God. Maybe if Sydney Jenkins—the ordinary child, not the pastor's daughter living life in a fishbowl—had not lacked the good luck to be born under a nameless star for those kids who just played softball and grew up to marry well and that was all there was to it, perhaps life might have included a God in there somewhere. With any luck, she might have passed through Sunday school with the little gray-haired teacher scarcely remembering her face. If Sydney could have wished for something large, it would have been to live life faceless.

One of Pierre Gaston's prostitutes lit a cigarette outside her window. Her dark hair hung around her face, flaccid, black curls making her look like a young child just bathed. She saw Sydney through the glass but turned away. Two young women followed her and never acknowledged Sydney.

"Be careful what you wish," the voice of Sydney's father whispered.

8

"I THOUGHT YOU TOOK the day off." Carol pushed herself back from the desk and followed Wade into his office. She held a tuna sandwich in her hand, double tomato, hold the mayo. "A little bird told me you were on the way. I bought you another bag of cough drops."

"Something has come up." His office felt small to him, more cluttered than he remembered it, almost as though he needed to clean it all out and reorganize every piece. "I have to fly out tonight to New Orleans." Wade stretched open his leather brief-case, a worn-out, age-softened case, and rummaged for a file.

"You're going after Sydney. It's about time, sir, if you don't mind my saying so. That girl has suffered long enough with that Ray fellow."

"Is there anything you don't know about, Carol?"

She rubbed the snow globe on her desk with her free hand like a seer. She smelled of tuna and office machinery, although when the air vents kicked on, she smelled more of baby powder, like women who use powder instead of deodorant.

"Better grab a pad and bring it with you—please. We have a lot to go over before I leave. I still haven't packed. I don't even know if I should do this. We're right in the middle of a Christmas pageant and the end-of-year report. We'll have to reschedule all those meetings. I guess I'm insane. Am I, Carol?"

She left the tuna sandwich on a napkin on her desk corner. "Oh, and Mrs. Huddleston's on her way here with Suzie."

"She knows I'm off today."

"Grace called your house. Isabella phoned here to warn you." She handed him the note. "She's the little bird."

"I can't let Grace take up my afternoon. Be insistent, will you—five minutes is all I can give her." Wade took his seat and lifted a pen from his penholder. He dropped it when the fire alarm sounded.

Carol sighed.

"Not this. Not now. You think this is for real, Carol?" He yelled to be heard over the alarm bell. He remembered the last false alarm, when one of the preschoolers had escaped from the nap room.

"For the life of me I don't know, Pastor. Better safe than sorry, I say. I see Ralph; he's evacuating the secretarial pool. Hey, do you smell that?"

"Smells like an electrical fire." He stuffed several files into his briefcase and snapped the flaps together. "Out you go."

Carol ran out of his office and into her front office to fumble through her file drawer for her handbag. She yelled for someone to fetch Nora from the copier room. Meticulous to a flaw, Carol wrapped the tuna sandwich in a napkin. "Has anyone seen my crackers? I know I had cheese and crackers right here next to this tuna sandwich."

Wade pressed his hands against both sides of his face in disbelief and then stepped around her.

Ralph Helmsley, the building super, dashed past. He hefted a large fire extinguisher over his head and led a parade of four maintenance men into the choir's practice and storage room. He was a wiry man, all red hair and ball cap, with fringes of sharp, red tufts forever pointed toward the nape of his neck. He had a northern Virginia twang that made the Floridian staff chuckle but made Wade feel like he was back home with the Tennesseans.

Smoke billowed out into the lobby. Two secretaries sat paralyzed, little butterflies caught in a net, until Carol coaxed them toward the nearest exit.

Wade hied after the maintenance crew. He yelled over his shoulder, "Carol, will you check the preschoolers? Better make sure Erma's got them all lined up and out of the building."

She nodded and disappeared down the hall, sans tuna salad and crackers.

The red light flashed first on line one and then line two while the answering machine at the secretaries' desk in the lobby took duty.

Carol's voice gurgled in a distant indiscernible dictum.

"Ralph, what's going on?" Wade stepped out of the way while another maintenance man, Henry, stumbled past. The young man, a Jersey transplant, coughed and covered his mouth with a pink chamois.

"Coffeepot in here must have shorted, Pastor." Ralph hosed down the semicharred wall while the others doused the partly melted lawn manger scene and the rack of Christmas costumes. Ralph veered in and around his crew, agile and nimble as a monkey. "Looks like we've contained it, Pastor."

"I'll go open some doors," Wade said. "What a mess. Looks like it damaged a lot of Christmas pageant props and costumes. Better send for Farris."

"I'll get the doors, Pastor!" Henry, the Jersey maintenance man, ran past.

"Is it safe to let everyone come back inside, Ralph?" Wade surveyed the room. Someone opened a window to let out the smoke.

"Sure can. We've shut off the breaker to this room. Reckon you won't have lights in the bathrooms up front. You'll have to use the east wing rest rooms until we get this wiring fixed."

"You and your guys did a fine job, Ralph." Wade leaned toward Ralph, clapped his shoulder with one hand, and shook his free hand with the other. They both smelled like a barbecue pit.

Just as Wade rounded the corner to his office, he saw Nora Maggert perched between the copier room and the reception desk, her eyes drawn into tiny beads as she assessed the empty clouded room. He opened his mouth to call out to her. But Nora withdrew, as though she had departed her own brittle shell, her face stricken with a peculiar angst.

"Victim inside!" Three firefighters barreled toward her, gigantic behemoths who saw only a frail victim left behind. As one swooped her into his arms, the others cried out for those who might yet remain inside the church.

"Wait, we've contained the fire!" Wade charged toward them.

Nora shrieked. Then she fainted. The tall firefighter rushed outdoors with what looked to be a boneless old woman held flaccid against his beefy frame.

Wade came within earshot of the other two men. "Over here! We've put out the fire!"

Ralph led the firemen into the choir room. Jersey Henry followed, eager for once to be in Florida.

WADE CONSIDERED all of the damaged Christmas props collected over the years punishment enough for Farris's covert habit of leaving the coffeepot turned on for hours on end. After the fire chief's summation, Carol called the insurance adjuster and then asked Henry to drive Nora home. The preschoolers—little ducks ready for naps amid a mosaic of terry-cloth pallets—filed in behind Erma.

"Pastor, we've got messages galore," Carol said while she adjusted the privacy curtains on the glass wall between her office and Wade's.

"Every meeting next week has to be rescheduled. No matter what, I'll be back Wednesday by noon. We can start with the year-end meeting late Wednesday night after the midweek service."

"They've pulled late-nighters before." Carol scribbled while Wade dictated. With one ear inclined toward the phone, she listened to the drone of the answering machine. "I'll call everyone back myself."

Farris paced outside Carol's office and gulped coffee.

"Tell Farris to stop worrying, for pete's sake!"

"Farris, stop worrying for pete's sake!" Carol cupped her hand to her mouth. Farris heard neither of them.

"He can get Rudy Wilkins to build a stable, a manger—"

"Two plastic cows and a sheep. Then there's the Mary and Joseph for the front lawn. . . ."

"All of this worry over props. I'm just thankful we contained the fire. No one was hurt. The Lord had his hand on us, that's what I say." Wade shoved papers into the briefcase, blank reports that he would painstakingly fill in on the flight.

"Nora had an exciting day, don't you think?" Carol took a hand sweeper to Wade's carpet even though the foot traffic from the fire had stopped at her door.

"She fainted dead away, if that's what you call exciting."

"I've never seen her so happy."

"Carol, that's absurd."

"She had some muscular young guy hauling her around like a rag doll. She couldn't wait to get home and phone all the ladies' gardening club members."

"So you think she really didn't faint."

"Women don't faint. That's a myth that men like to believe. Have you ever fainted? Oh, I'm sorry, Pastor. I didn't mean—"

"You shouldn't listen to rumors."

"You didn't faint in front of Breyers Ice Cream, then?"

"I thought it was a heart attack. It could have been serious."

"Of course, sir." She accentuated each word in an "attaboy" fashion.

"Carol, I don't know if you've ever had an epiphany, but what happened to me this morning just might have saved my life."

"Oh, I should call the prayer chain. 'Scratch prayers for pastor's heart attack. Pray for his, what, epiphany'?"

"You're fired."

"Again!"

"But not until we've finished this list."

"Then I get to go home."

"No, you need to stay on, see that the meetings are all rescheduled and that—"

"What's wrong, sir? Are you all right? It's just a kid, it sounds like, on the answering machine. Probably got the wrong number."

"Rewind it, Carol, please! I know that voice."

She rewound the message.

A child cleared his throat, stammered, then said, "Grandpa, it's me. Mommy, we got us this room—" he stopped, intermittent pauses punctuated with whispers as though he were not alone— "but it's not a nice place and you need to come get us. Corette, the lady with pink hair, she's a nice lady and I think she does tricks or something. Like, maybe she's a magician—"

"It's Trevor! I know it's him!" Wade blanched.

"—but I don't like it and Mommy, she cries. But Allie likes it, but I don't. So come and get us. It's at the long road with big trucks. . . ."

Life swished past Wade, a parade of emotions that left him gutted as he waited for Trevor to provide the final clue to their whereabouts.

". . . Mommy's coming. I got to go. Bye, Grandpa. I'll be waiting by the window. Tell Grammy to make chocolate gravy. It's raining here. Allie has a fever. Bye."

A gulf breeze stirred the orange hibiscus outside the pastor's study.

"Trevor, tell Grandpa where you are." Wade whispered it.

"YOU'RE SUCH A BIG GUY to remember where she left it." Sydney took the doll from Trevor and tucked it next to Allie. "If she woke up and found that smelly old doll gone, she'd really be upset." Sydney had sent Trevor with her set of motel keys back to the last room to find the doll. From the window, she watched him enter. He stayed a little too long. Torn between leaving Allie alone and running to fetch him, she had waited a few minutes past her patience when he appeared. "You're wet."

"I brought Allie's toy bag. She left all her toys in the room." Trevor climbed up onto the foldout bed. "I'll save them for her."

"That's nice of you, Trevor." Sydney dumped the contents of her purse onto the bed. "Here it is. Allie's medicine for fever."

"I didn't take it, Mommy!"

"Of course you didn't. It was here in my purse all along."

"I don't want you to be mad at me."

"Trevor, are you all right, honey?"

The boy nodded, openmouthed.

"Go get your sister's cup and fill it with water. Allie, wake up, sweetie."

Trevor cupped his hands beneath a slight lump in his shirt.

"I'M SORRY, SIR. I'll call the operator. Maybe we can trace the number through the phone service."

"Isabella was right. I was wrong. Sydney and the kids are in trouble. A lady who does tricks—that's a prostitute, Carol."

"You're fast, Pastor. I'm thinking they've joined a circus, but you—I'll bet you're right."

"I'll call Isabella and see if she has a flight out yet."

"She does, sir. It was message number six, right here. See?"

"Eight o'clock out of Tampa Bay with a layover in Atlanta." He scribbled it down.

"I'll get you a room at the Wyndham New Orleans. After you find them, you'll want to take them to a nice place."

"And a rental car. I'm forgetting something."

"Grace Huddleston."

"No, not Grace."

"I mean, she's looking at us through the glass. Grace and Suzie. Oh, and Buzz. Poor guy, but you play, you pay. Here, have a cough drop."

"I can't deal with the Huddlestons today. Please tell them we've had a full-blown emergency. Grace can see all of those firemen milling around. Tell her I'll see her next Thursday. Tell her anything." He closed his door.

Wade felt haunted, as though he moved too slowly, as though he had moved too slowly all along. He was a big Galápagos turtle that sunned on the beach while the seals got eaten by sharks. And his daughter and grandchildren were the seals.

Sydney feels alienated. He almost said it aloud. She must, or why else would she not call him? Alienation had been a parenting tool for his own parents—the silent treatment, shaking of the head, the disappointed glances. He had responded in decent and proper fashion as a son. Sydney was an opposite pole. In a long line of manipulators, she had emerged the girl with a trusting nature, a positive outlook, a merciful demeanor. Years of applying the measures he thought would toughen her, wisen her, had slipped off her chamois-buffed ideology. She pressed him into his fatherly corner, made him keep talking until the right answer came out of him. It always made him sigh. Sometimes he retaliated with his big "male" guns—a weighty silence that said, "I'm disappointed."

Carol peered in while she rapped against his door. She thrust in her head. "Sir, we have a situation. The Huddlestons ask for only five minutes."

Grace stood behind Carol and held up five fingers. Her stretched smile coupled with Suzie's wide-eyed stare caused the two of them to look like two paper dolls propped against the plate-glass dividing wall.

The Huddlestons filed past him with the nervous groom on Suzie's heels.

"Pastor, I don't know if anyone has ever told you this but you look like Robert DeNiro." Grace cut the air with her hand and made up-and-down motions in front of him as though she were slicing tomatoes.

"Grace, Suzie. Nice to see you again, Buzz."

The collegiate shook his hand. "Nice to see you, Pastor Jenkins."

"Have a seat. Carol told you I have to leave soon. We're in a bit of a situation here and I have to clear up some matters before I leave."

"I was so surprised to see all the firefighters. Nora told us all about the excitement and how she was rescued by that handsome young man. He should get a medal."

"Mom, stop with the stuff about Nora. Pastor, I don't know if you know, but I'm expecting a baby—we, Buzz and me, we're expecting a baby."

Wade clasped his hands in front of his chest.

"Suzie and me, we need to get married right away," said Buzz.

"I still say you did this on purpose," said Grace. "Pastor, I just got one wedding paid for and asked these two to wait a year. But do they listen?"

"If you hadn't interfered, we would be married by now and I wouldn't be in this fix, Mother."

"This is the thanks, this is the thanks," said Grace.

"Well, if you want to finish your premarital counsel, the soonest I can see you is next Thursday."

"Counsel? We don't need any more counsel, Pastor. We want to get married today."

"I'm sorry, Suzie. I don't arrange ceremonies that quickly. If you want a justice of the peace, you can go downtown. At Clearwater Freewill we have a procedure for couples—first comes the premarital counsel. I've met with you three times. When I return from New Orleans we'll finish the last session and then take a look at the calendar."

"Pastor, I'm close to second trimester. If I wait so much as another week, I won't be able to wear my grandmother's wedding gown. It's tradition. I have to wear it." Tears the size of Wade's knuckles slid down her face. "We don't need anything else. We got the flowers, the unity candle, and the Wedding Songs for Lovers music cassette from Wal-Mart."

Buzz nodded, more of a nervous gesture. He kept an uneasy eye out for Grace. "I picked it up at Wal-Mart this morning."

"Buzz, how do you feel about this . . . rushed ceremony?" Wade slid the briefcase off the desktop and set it beside him. He was ready to go.

"I love Suzie, Mr.—Pastor, that is. We just need to hurry it up a little, is all."

Wade's shoulders lifted.

"Counsel? What counsel could they need? They've figured out all the secret stuff," said Grace.

"Counsel is for later, Grace. When things get tough," said Wade.

"Mother, you don't need to be here. You'll just muck everything up." Suzie toyed with the Mary and Joseph figurines that were displayed on one corner of Wade's desk.

"Mrs. Beaman said you were leaving, Pastor. May I ask at what time?" Grace patted Suzie's knee, a ginger tap that said it was time for a mother's intervention.

"To get through traffic, arrive by seven at the American Airlines terminal at Tampa International—I have to be on the interstate by six-fifteen."

"You all still have to sign for your marriage license, right, kids?" Grace asked.

"Marriage license?" Buzz had a smattering of freckles that darkened when he blushed.

Suzie squeezed Buzz's hand. "We did that already. This morning. When you signed your name at the courthouse."

"Oh," said Buzz.

"I still haven't packed, Grace. That's why I have to leave now." Wade made a move toward the door and said a silent prayer, a hope that he would blink his eyes and they would all disappear.

"Suzie, you said Buzz and you wanted a nontraditional wedding. You could marry right at the airport, right before Pastor leaves." Grace locked her jaw with her mouth open.

"But I wanted the unity candle." Suzie's hand slipped inside Buzz's heavy one.

"Grace, you aren't serious. Suzie and Buzz deserve a better ceremony. I'll be back Wednesday. They can get married on Thursday. Loren Matthews can fill you all in on the final counseling session. I trained him myself. Suzie, tell your mother you can wait." Wade squared his shoulders and pushed himself back from the desk.

"This could be, like, a really big deal. If we tell the television stations we're getting married in an airport, I'll bet they'll tape it and air it on *Larry Guinn's Magic Moments*." Suzie had a look of deep satisfaction.

"I think they pay you for that," Buzz said. "We could use it to put money down on a trailer."

Grace came to her feet. "We can stop by Pastor Matthews's office on the way out to finish up the, what you call it, the last counseling session. I'll call the airport and see what the regulations say about weddings and candles and such. This is Florida, Pastor Jenkins. Anything is possible."

9

"THIS IS FOOLISH, Isabella. How I got mixed up in this sort of thing, I'll never know."

"Carol told me how you solved all those problems today, Wade. She called you 'the master' at calming the troubled waters. And now you're going off to rescue Sydney and the kids. I told Carol I had to agree—you are an amazing guy."

"Don't say 'rescue.' Everyone will hear."

"Oh, even the television people know our daughter's missing. Ted Gandy called the house and asked for an exclusive. Can you believe it—me, doing an exclusive?"

"You shouldn't have told him anything, Isabella. For all we know, Sydney's lolling around a fireplace with friends sipping hot chocolate and not giving a thought to how we might be sick with worry over her."

"Wade, the cameras are rolling. Smile." Isabella spoke through bared teeth.

"The cameras are rolling? My own wife has gone Hollywood. Next thing you know, we'll be staging baptisms and communion. Let's make stars of everyone, why don't we?"

"It's good press, Wade. And you've made Suzie and Buzz so happy. What might have been a prickly situation for them, you've made into a happy memory."

"I thought I was supposed to leave town quietly. Now the whole church will hear that I succumbed to marrying these two headstrong teenage parents-to-be and I'm off on a mission to fetch back our wayward daughter and grandkids."

"More people to pray for us, that's all." Isabella glanced at the wedding party.

"And once again, the Jenkinses take another lap around the aquarium."

"Anyway, Buzz and Suzie messed up but they sure can't change their situation now. They need our help, Wade, not our condemnation. And Sydney's not wayward. Not like some families have wayward children. I mean, look what Grace has to deal with right now. No, Sydney just married into waywardness, like some people just fall into bad luck. That sounds good—I'll say it to Ted just like that."

Watch them swim round the bend, thought Wade. *No secrets with this family! They should put that in the seminary playbook—oh, and we should mention that as a pastor you are signing away all rights to privacy.*

Three young college girls fussed around Suzie Huddleston, applying powder and lipstick and straightening the tulle around her crown. A television camera lens aimed square into her face. She glanced at it from time to time, giggled, and then fell back into the blithe wedding chatter among her admiring club of bridesmaids.

"Look, Wade. A jet is docking. I'll bet that's your flight." Isabella adjusted the silk scarf at her throat.

Wade cleared the knot from his own throat. "If everyone is ready, all of you in the wedding party can take your places." Wade remained stiff, almost grave, while Grace Huddleston pinned him with a white carnation. She sniffed twice and then burst into tears.

The local television broadcasting celebrity, Ted Gandy, waited for the countdown—his cue—and then explained in a hushed tone how a local pastor caught in the throes of a family crisis had solved the problems of an eager young couple by agreeing to marry them before he himself embarked on a journey to New Orleans. Travelers stopped to gawk and point at Pastor Wade Jenkins.

"He's off to rescue his daughter. She's missing, you know."

"It could be a kidnapping. Those ministers make big bucks, some of them."

Wade sighed and felt his ears redden. He would hear it all replayed on the golf green and never hear the end of it. Mentally, he disappeared onto a quiet knoll for a moment while the crowd thickened around them. Isabella was prodded into place next to Gandy, an attractive blush upon her cheeks as she asked for prayers for their family. He owed it to himself to play a round, he told himself—*once I get this little mess with Sydney cleared up. It shouldn't take long. We'll be back soon, our family safe and sound as it should be.*

∽⟡∾

"WHAT IS THAT BEEPING NOISE? It's driving me crazy," said Sydney. She dug through Allie's toy bag. Some battery-operated gadget had been left on. She could hear it.

"I don't hear a beeping." Trevor stood up on his knees. He watched the rain through the window above the full bed. "Birds don't fly south around here," he said. He watched a flock of dark birds descend on some crumbs swept out after breakfast.

"Don't tell me you don't hear the beeping, Trevor. You hear every little peep, every noise, and you don't hear it?"

Sydney waited, studying Trevor's pensive gaze. Nothing but the tapping radio made a sound.

"Nope. Nothing." Trevor went back to bird-watching. "If you wait until almost dark, those two ladies come out without their coats on from that room. They'll catch a cold just like Allie if they don't watch out."

Allie stirred. The redness had faded from her cheeks, restoring her face to its cool, milky color. Sydney knelt on one knee next to her bed and bowed her head. She whispered, "Thank you."

"You're talking to God," said Trevor.

"I'm not talking to anyone. I don't know what you mean," she said.

Trevor reacted when the birds, startled by a rainy wind, lifted in front of the window, spiraled one behind the other, and filled the air outside the Budget Palace with irate bird twittering. The boy lifted his arms and spiraled down to the full bed.

The annoying sound chirped again.

Sydney blew out a breath. "I guess you didn't hear that, either."

"It's just birds, Mommy." He had an odd smile.

"GET THIS, WILL YOU?" Carol handed a note to Vera Klumb, a secretary who acted as an aide to Carol.

"What is it?" Vera asked.

"I've been trying to trace the number from where that little Trevor Oliver called."

"I hope you found that poor child."

"It's a puzzle, Vera. An outright puzzle. They traced the number to a mobile phone. The operator says it's listed with a Reverend Hank DeLucey."

"Maybe Sydney's been taken in by a church. You think?"

"That would be wonderful, Vera. But I've been calling this number and all I get is a recording saying the customer is away or some such."

"Why not give me a few minutes and I'll keep trying it while you tidy up all the other jobs Pastor Jenkins left for you? No need to pull another all-nighter. Too many of those lately. I want to go home and get ready for my grandkids."

"Vera, you're a peach. You call me the minute you get an answer."

Vera pranced away, invigorated by the chase of the hunt.

"A pastor," Carol said to herself. "I don't get this at all."

10

"PASSENGERS, we will land shortly and arrive at our destination at New Orleans International. We ask that you stow all loose items under the seat in front of you and return your seat to its upright and locked position. . . ."

"I guess you've been to a wedding."

All but settled into a semipeaceful slumber, Wade shook himself, blinked, and lifted his eyes to acknowledge the middle-aged woman seated next to him. "Pardon me?"

"I said, I guess you've been to a wedding." She pointed toward his carnation, then blinked at him with green eyes that reminded him of a throw pillow given to Isabella by Nora—a sort of faded green. "Thyme," Isabella had called it, although he never thought of thyme when he saw it—just Nora's Kmart perfume.

"Oh, the flower. Forgot I had it on."

"And rice." She flicked two grains from his shoulder. It jarred him to have a strange woman raid his comfort zone. She must have just applied a red-orange lipstick. Her smile revealed a smudged trail of the almost phosphorescent red across her two front teeth.

"I just married a couple." He retrieved the rice from his lap and tucked it into his pocket. "This young pair back in Tampa Bay had this crazy idea of having an airport wedding. That's back before, I guess, you boarded in Atlanta."

"Gee, I'm sorry I missed it. I almost missed this flight. I noticed you were already asleep when I took my seat. I hated to disturb you, but we are about to land."

Wade shrugged. "Not to worry."

"So you fly around marrying people, then?"

"No. I'm a pastor back in Clearwater. I have to fly to New Orleans. . . . It's a long story. You off visiting family, I guess?"

"My son and his wife. They live in Metairie, so close I told them not to bother picking me up. Pretty little community too. Not all dirty like New Orleans—not that I'm at all disparaging the city. It's just that cities are not for me. I live outside Atlanta, even. I guess, for some, New Orleans has its charm."

"Take in a horse-and-carriage ride and then taxi on over to Ralph and Kacoo's—good food, and you'll get a better feel for the town."

"Now that sounds like fun. You ought to join me."

"I have business. Sorry."

She sat in an awkward silence while Wade focused his attention through the window. The airplane circled in a somnolent arc, first gliding over the evening lights of New Orleans and then enter-

ing the lightless realm above the deep, still darkness of Lake
Pontchartrain with the causeway crossing its heart like a zipper.

"I didn't mean that like a date. No offense, Reverend."

"No, ma'am. No offense taken." He felt the thud of the wheels
as the pilot engaged the landing gear, as though the bowels of the
craft had dropped out and spilled onto the historical rooftops
below.

"You do look kind of good-looking, not like some pastors, but
more like Robert DeNiro. I guess you hear that a lot."

Wade slid out an old issue of *Time* and thumbed through it.
Isabella had stuffed the periodical into the pocket of his briefcase
just in case he had a moment to read.

"I am a widow, but far be it from me to try and take a pastor
on a date. But I make friends easily, I'm told."

He shifted onto his left hip and pointed his right shoulder toward
the window. By his silence, he offered the woman a hasty farewell.

She muttered something to herself, then fell silent.

An article about New Orleans caught his eye. According to the
journalist, the future of the City on a Swamp, which was situated
below sea level, teetered on the dangerous premise that it might
someday crumble into the sea. Considered an island, the city of
New Orleans for centuries had operated as an undisturbed, self-reli-
ant society, all but unreachable by the outside world or explorers
and inhabited by over seventy different ethnic groups—all of that
accounting for its European flavor. Not until 1800 did a bridge-
building project finally connect the Big Easy with the infant coun-
try that had purchased it.

He considered Sydney and the cosmic hole that separated him
from his daughter. He shut his eyes, prayerful that an even greater

bridge could span the opposite poles of their emotions and traverse the gap between them. But first of all, he had to find her.

THE COMING WINTER SOLSTICE left no mark on the Crescent City of New Orleans, no hoary stinging breath upon the face of the evening pedestrian who scrambled from curb to cab, no icy sky to hold the earth captive in a wintry freeze, no frost to kill the summer pests. The New Orleans winter heralded the spirit of Mardi Gras, which the city was renowned for and ushered in crawfish season, and King Cakes, and purple and yellow lights strung in cozy windows of families named Guitreau and Soileau. Airport shopwindows displayed children's books with alligators dressed as St. Nick, books that told tales of Cajun Christmases and gifts delivered down the bayou in long pirogues by Papa Noel.

Store shelves, lined with beignet mix and chicory coffee, glittered with purple, green, and gold beads alongside traditional Christmas stockings. Isabella had handed Wade a list of items to bring home, but he felt too weary to pull it out.

He carted his luggage through the line of rental car booths, picked up the automobile key reserved by Carol, and made his way toward the exit. He braced himself for the cold, as he had done on many occasions when he traveled away from Florida in the winter. But instead, the muggy, tropical air warmed his senses as he traversed the rows along the car rental lot, counted, and then stopped behind slot number thirteen. Carol had requested a practical, sensible car—at least that was the message she had sent to his e-mail box. He paced behind slot number thirteen and wondered how the bright red Camaro translated into "practical." A convertible, no less. Isabella would have leaped into the driver's seat at first sight of it. The number on the coded key chain matched the car number exactly. He heaved a sigh and felt around in his jacket until he found the map that Carol had printed for him from the Internet.

"Nice car. At least you had the good sense to call ahead. They told me you got the last one. It's getting harder and harder to get a car rental."

The sound of the Atlanta woman's voice unnerved Wade. He maintained his poise and turned to face her. "I'm sorry. It's only because my secretary takes care of everything. I can call you a cab if that would help."

"I'll call a cab. You need help with your map?"

"Carol has it all on here."

She put on a pair of eyeglasses and then studied the pen markings Carol had scrawled on the paper. "This Carol, she's from New Orleans?"

"No, but she's efficient."

"You're headed for Jackson Square?"

"No, not exactly. It's an apartment complex—the Lafreniere Apartments on Dauphine Street."

"She's got you headed the wrong way. My kids have friends on that street. I can give you better directions, if you want. But I don't want to be a bother to you, Pastor. You don't want to get lost in that part of town late at night, if you know what I mean."

"Mrs.—"

"Charlotte Myers." She extended her hand. "I just hate to see you get lost downtown this late." She had Carol's smile, an organized mien about her.

"I'm sorry if I was rude on the plane. I have a lot to accomplish on this trip. I tend to get overfocused, or at least my wife thinks so."

"Not to worry. You want me to write this down for you? Then I should go. I have to catch my cab."

A soft mist started to fall. Wade felt guilty that he had taken the last rental car and treated a stranger with so little regard. He knew what Sydney would say about him. "Tell you what, Mrs. Myers—you get me some better directions and I'll give you a lift to Metairie. Looks like, according to the map anyway, that I can drop you off along the way."

"I hate to put you to the trouble, Pastor."

"No, I insist. It's the least I can do to make up for my, well, to show a little kindness to a stranger. You have luggage?"

"I only have this one carry-on." Small beads of mist formed on her lenses. She looked like an insect, something large with unexpected wings.

"All right, then. Let's get out of this drizzle."

She gathered the small carry-on piece beneath one arm and walked toward the passenger side of the Camaro.

Wade recalled a small detail about something she had said on the flight. He had gotten the impression she knew nothing about New Orleans. Instead, she was a godsend, more knowledgeable about the area than he had ascertained.

He permitted himself to feel grateful.

CORETTE SAT IN THE ROOM while the kids slept, lolling in a chair with her feet tucked beneath her, leonine fashion, her eyes lambent in the glow of the television. She sat mesmerized in front of the Home Shopping Network while Sydney finished making up the rooms. It had rained all day, and the kids had slept through dinner.

Sydney hauled the cleaning cart into her room. "I'm done, Corette. Good. They're still asleep."

"You have yourself two angels, that's what." Corette left to preen and have a smoke; it was only an hour before the cars would parade into the parking lot of the Budget Palace.

Sydney ordered a home delivery pizza but let Trevor and Allie sleep while she drew their evening bath. She dribbled liquid bath soap beneath the running faucet and watched the crème turn from lactescence to foam. She closed her eyes. The floral soap smelled extravagant, like a spa. Two white Turkish towels hung from her cart. A glass dish full of votive candles was reserved for the Business Package rooms. She unfolded the towels and placed them on the small table beside the bathtub. Then she lit two of the candles and placed one at each end of the tub. In half a minute, she undressed and slid into the foaming water. With one hand she increased the force of the water, while with the other she squeezed out a more generous amount of soap beneath the faucet. The water rose over her shoulders and up to her neck. Her muscles still ached from stooping over the beds of strangers, but she felt delicious and alone. Wounded but safe.

Ray came to her mind, and as often as she chased him away, he settled inside her—but at a safe distance, so that she could study his pain. As the memory of him came into view, his colors rose to the surface like pieces bobbing up after the sinking of a ship. She reenacted their last fight. He had fired his petty jussives at her as though he expected her to roll over.

Marriage was a domestic device for him, an asylum he could crawl into after he had forced himself through the sieve of daylight, only to return home in pieces. Sydney was the caretaker of this asylum's mechanism—at least in his estimation. Her vows brought her into his world, the small universe that surrounded Ray and kept him in his orbit. She was but another piece of that orbit, a small moon or something smaller. When she broke a law, she paid.

Sydney turned off the faucet and sunk up to her chin. Inside her mind, her father was walking into the room and standing next to Ray. He had a list of Ray's flaws—the list she never wanted to read. She forced her father to toss the list and just look at her. She wanted him to see her imperfections wound up with the rest of her, to see the parts of her that other people admired but that he never acknowledged. Dad had never been able to embrace all of her, but rather just the presentable parts, the ones that looked good to his church. So in their last two years, he had never embraced any of her at all. Ray and Wade, side by side, had nothing in common. Yet now everything came clear and she saw the sickness of it all. She was an object, a moon, a reflecting pool to two souls—one erudite, the other imperceptive—two souls who expected her to echo their expectations. But when her life possessed only the power to hark back their own inadequacies, they pronounced her fractured and worthless.

The water covered her lips. She let the air flow from her nostrils and, for a moment, she felt as slight as a pet-store turtle with the pond of the universe surrounding her. Wade and Ray disappeared from her thoughts. Two tears tumbled into the water and summoned deeper things—things larger, invisible, and reaching out to her. She suddenly felt acknowledged but not examined.

More tears fell, and she felt her body heave. Trevor, a light sleeper, might hear. She permitted herself a gentle cry. Sydney knew that deafness to God was self-imposed and yet, when she succumbed to brokenness, suddenly things unheard were comprehensible. She could hear something as deep as a godlike whisper; it drummed against her fallow heart like gentle rain.

She stayed until the water grew tepid, until all was quiet and she could dismiss the last few minutes as nothing more than a moment of peaceful hysteria.

11

THE RAIN SUBSIDED. Giddy laughter echoed from the parking lot. Three of Pierre's women engaged a few men in scatty talk, forming a small impromptu beer party beneath the neon office sign. Plastic lanterns and Christmas lights made an overhead web across the lot from the office to the rooms. The girls had donned body-tight dresses: floral print, ruffled at the shoulders, their bare arms covered by lacy shawls.

Acadian women all had hair as black as sleek panthers, but curled, rings of silk about their faces. Smooth olive skin with dark brows underscored the bright fabrics they wore and the bloodred lip color. One of them had turned up a radio in a Business Package room and left the door standing open. A recording from a Cajun band played from the cheap sound system. Cajun music possessed its own jolting rhythm, a sound that moved dancing feet across wooden floors, tapping, a marching jig with arms entwined and bodies twirling, first graceful and then regimented.

But these girls lacked the full brilliance of other Acadians. Like wilted flowers clinging to the stem, they paraded through the night, marcescent and only half alive.

Two of the women appeared drunk already. Sydney pulled the blinds closed.

Trevor finished his pizza and asked how many days until Christmas.

"Not long, sweetie," said Sydney.

"We should send a letter to Santa and let him know we're here." Trevor pushed aside his paper plate.

Allie ate only a few bites of cheese pizza.

"Trevor, I promise we won't be here through Christmas. I found some better jobs in the newspaper today. Corette might stay with you all tomorrow while I go for interviews."

"Santa might never find us if we keep moving. Allie needs a new doll."

Allie hugged the rag doll close to her. "No!"

"Trevor, Santa won't lose track of us. Allie, you could use a new doll. Let me see that one. She has a torn leg."

"She hurt herself running away," said Allie.

"Running from what?"

"Daddy." Allie covered the doll with the sheet. "All she needs is a Band-Aid."

"Those people are loud," said Trevor. "Grammy wouldn't like those women."

Sydney stopped short of saying, "Those women wouldn't like Grammy either."

"I'm bored. You don't read to us anymore, Mommy." The boy blinked, his mouth a small outline of a smile.

She paused. "When we find a good place to live, we'll buy more books for you, Trevor."

"In this drawer, I found a book." He opened the nightstand drawer. From inside the drawer, he lifted a Gideon Bible.

"That's not a storybook, Trevor. It's too hard for kids to understand."

"No, it's the Christmas story. Grandpa reads us the story every Christmas."

"Let's watch a movie instead." Sydney picked up the remote control.

"When Grandpa comes, he can read it to us," said Trevor.

"Go wash your hands and then climb into bed. I'll read it." Sydney opened the hardback Bible. It had crisp new pages except for one page, which was dog-eared at the top right corner. Sydney opened the page and smoothed it. Her eye fell on some red text:

"Who touched My clothes?"

The words of Christ leaped out at her. She read the passage surrounding it and remembered from her childhood the story of a woman healed by touching Christ's clothing. The miracle stood out on its own merit. But what struck her was how one touch had drawn the attention of God. A throng of people surrounded him; yet he had focused all of his attention on one woman, noticed by no one but him.

"Did you find the Christmas story?" asked Trevor.

"I'm still looking." Sydney slid the Bible ribbon out and marked the place between the pages of the text she had just read. "Okay. I found it."

The music grew louder outside. Sydney cleared her throat and read loud enough to overcome the sound of the revelers:

"'So it was, that while they were there, the days were completed for her to be delivered. And she brought forth her first-born Son, and wrapped Him in swaddling cloths, and laid Him in a manger, because there was no room for them in the inn. . . .'"

CHARLOTTE MYERS HANDED written directions to Wade. "I find that writing out the directions helps better than following one of those Internet maps. For instance, those streets right there—they're not actually blocked off like that. The streets wind round to follow the curve of the Mississippi." The streetlights illuminated her face in intermittent flickers. "These directions here will actually get you where you're going. You'll find the Lafreniere Apartments right behind this building. Take this alley right beside this bar—you'll see people out in the streets with Hurricanes, but don't worry about that—it's a safe area because it's a tourist hot spot. Then on to this street, to this street, and there you'll be."

"You seem to know a lot about New Orleans."

"My son's friends live near Dauphine Street, that's all. Ever been to a crawfish boil?"

"Can't say I have."

"The Cajuns, they set up big boiling pots right out in their front yards and have parties with crawfish, corn on the cob, these really spicy hot potatoes. My son's friends had a big crawfish boil right near Dauphine Street. They spread newspapers over outdoor tables and just pour the food right on the table. No utensils or plates. Just dig in. They know how to eat here in N'awlins. Here's my exit."

"I guess we tourists will never sample that side of New Orleans. Just the restaurant fare, is all."

She guided him past several streets and straight into Metairie. Damp moss hung from the large oak trees, spindly filaments that hung from gnarled branches—spidery veils by night beneath the streetlights, delicate antique lace by daylight. Charlotte guided him onto a quiet street, older homes framed all around with shrubs and trees and only one or two neighbors that had not extinguished the lights for the evening.

"You can turn into this drive on the right." She pulled out a cellular phone. "I'll call them and wake them so they can let me in. Thank you, Pastor, for the lift."

"Sure, Mrs. Myers."

"Please, that sounds so old. Charlotte is fine—if ever we meet again."

"Have a wonderful visit with your family." He wanted her to know by his tone that he would never meet her again.

"The directions are right here on the seat. You take care. Stay out of the cemeteries."

"I've heard about the cemeteries. You couldn't pay me to go into one at night." Carol and Isabella had harped on the cemeteries so much it had irritated him. *A haven for robbers*"—Isabella had let it be the last thing she said to him.

Wade watched Charlotte Myers take a few steps up the drive and then, phone to ear, she waved him on. The Acadian-styled neighborhood was a setting redolent of safe haven, he reasoned. He checked the traffic, turned the wheel, and might have offered a farewell gesture but realized that she had already disappeared. The house that belonged to her son retained its dark pall, no sign that anyone roused from his sleep to welcome a late-night visitor. Charlotte Myers had vanished. Wade blew out a breath. It was no longer his problem. He had delivered the woman to her self-appointed destination. He had to yank his thoughts back to task so that he could concentrate, make a plan, find Sydney and the kids. This Charlotte Myers could certainly fend for herself.

A STOP BY THE WYNDHAM New Orleans revealed that he had misunderstood Carol. The front desk clerk telephoned the other Wyndham Hotel and then pulled out a small commercial city map and sketched out a route for Wade with a black marker. "Not to worry, Pastor Jenkins. It happens all the time. We're not too far from the other hotel."

"Shame. You all are right here on the water too."

"You'll find the other Wyndham to your liking too. It's a fine hotel. You'll find the room accommodations exquisite."

Wade accepted the map and stuffed it into his briefcase to add to his growing collection of maps and directions. "If I get lost now, I'm a fool," he said.

The clerk offered a tacit nod.

"If you have a men's room, I'd like to freshen up, make a phone call if I may."

"Right down this hallway, Reverend Jenkins."

By Florida's time, it would be an hour later, almost midnight. But he knew Isabella well enough to know she'd be waiting by the phone all night if he didn't call. She answered right away. Wade cradled the phone against one ear while he washed his hands.

"Wade, I'm so glad you called. Carol has some news. According to the operator, the phone Trevor called from is a cell phone registered with, of all people, a pastor in New Orleans."

"Did Carol reach the pastor?"

"Tried all day. Even tried to get a home phone number, but it's not listed."

"He probably lives out in the suburbs. Carol would have to know the name of the township. Give me his name and I'll search the yellow pages. Sometimes the church ads will offer the pastor's name."

"I thought exactly the same thing. His name is Hank DeLucey."

Wade begged a yellow pages directory from the clerk and carried it out to the Camaro. Under the hotel parking-lot lights, he pored over the church pages. Finally, his finger slid down the last column, where a large display advertisement caught his eye. "International Outreach Community Church, Pastor Hank DeLucey. Thank you, Lord." He scribbled the phone number and address into his Day-Timer and returned the phone book to the clerk.

At the most, he might reach a volunteer manning the prayer line. He would have to wait until morning to call Pastor DeLucey. Charlotte Myers's directions lay on the passenger seat. He picked up the notepaper. One of the street names sounded familiar. He must have passed it coming in off the interstate. Before checking in at the Bourbon New Orleans Wyndham, he could swing by and see if Ray Oliver was home. Or if neighbors happened to be coming home late, he could ask them if they knew anything about a Pastor DeLucey who might have assisted Sydney. If he could square away just one bit of information, he might sleep with less worry.

Some of the streetlights along the Vieux Carre were dark. He turned onto Decatur and then followed Charlotte's directions until he came to a darkened building. A dim streetlight flickered, illuminating the ornate filigree ironwork along the balcony in a yellow haze. Her handwriting had directed him to take the alley between the two buildings. The drizzle had stopped. He locked the Camaro and looked up and down the streets for signs of a bar, people walking around with Hurricanes, a sign that indicated he had found the apartment building. Just beyond the alley, he saw a young woman stride past the alley's end. Car keys jingled from her hands as though she were leaving from home. Wade followed her up the alley. If he could catch her, she might know Sydney or direct him to the Lafreniere Apartments.

The narrow alley emptied out into another alley. He thought he saw a bit of clothing flicker and then disappear at the next corner. Once again he ran after her. He called out, "Excuse, me! Miss!"

Dark walls of brick rose above him, towers that blocked his way. Wade ran and felt his feet lift and fall slow and tarantula-like against the partially cobbled alley. Nothing like his high school days when staying in shape had everything to do with youthfulness. The alley opened out into a field. In the distance, he heard a drunk droning out a pathetic version of "Jingle Bells." His shoe slammed against a stone and he felt his knee bend against his will. Crumpled against the ground, Wade's face and right shin burned as though scraped. When he reached up, his fingers detected indentations in the weathered marble. The winter moon illuminated the headstone in a milky veil. He strained to read the writing but could only make out the date of December 18, 1898. Isabella had told him to stay away from the cemeteries. The sound of running feet behind him caused him to call out again just before a sharp pain shot across the back of his head and down his neck. The cool prickle of graveyard grass stabbed his face. He heard nothing more.

12

SYDNEY AWOKE at ten o'clock that night. Everything became clear. She had lost herself in Ray's world. She had not told the truth about herself in two years, long enough to reinvent a new Sydney who found acceptance among the wives of the factory workers—Ray's collective pack of friends whose lives swiveled around the dictates of the metals industry of Louisiana. She awoke from her sleep on Friday night to realize that she loathed the smell of tobacco and empty six-packs, the odor of chemicals embedded in a man's cotton shirt.

Ray's troubles had fostered the pack of bill collectors who hounded them. But she had not been blind to his slow descent into the lesser being who wallowed in his problems as though he had finally come home to them. Not the heroic creature that he had painted himself up to be when they met on the campus at LSU, he now dropped words on her that distressed her.

"Stop waiting on me. Just do whatever you need to do to help out. I can't see straight right now. Just do whatever you need to do. Don't wait on me." He had given up on himself. He had given up on them.

Corette rapped at the window, a soft rapping not so brash as the Corette that paraded into those rooms at night. Sydney let her in, still dressed for the day in denims and a T-shirt.

"I brought this basket of clean sheets and pillowcases by for you, chère. I got a customer coming tonight, so, me, I better hurry. We got lots of business tonight, so you may want to start early tomorrow." Soft, white ashes floated down from the cigarette poised in the corner of her mouth. Corette jerked her head whenever she made a suggestion, as though she had been slapped for offering up her own ideas. "In the morning, you can wash all the other linens in the laundry room behind Pierre's office, like I told you before. You be sure and do up your own laundry while you're at it. Saves money and you don't have to go around with all that janglin' pocket change for the coin-op."

"Allie still has this terrible cough. I gave her some cough syrup. But she still feels warm."

Corette lifted Allie's limp hand to her face and pressed her lips against the child's skin. "You right about that. This baby's got herself a fever, but good. You mentioned your husband's job at the plant. He has good insurance, eh?"

"Did have. He lost his job."

"I can show you how to sign up for Medicaid."

"Medicaid."

"Don't you let no pride get in the way of takin' care of these kids."

Sydney pulled the covers all the way up to Allie's chin.

"You still haven't told me much about who you once was. Your daddy must be a rich man or somethin'."

"I'm a pastor's daughter, Corette."

"I don't know nothing about religion."

"It's less about religion. More about expectations. People expected me to fill some immaculate role. You just wake up one morning and realize you've forgotten what you look like, is all."

"I don't care what people say about me."

"I used to say that. Once, I admitted to a group of girls at church that I watched some movie. They were all talking about this movie, this stupid movie they had all seen. All but one talked about this film, so I just mentioned that I had seen it too. This one girl's mother was really strict and she barged into my father's office and demanded to know why he didn't keep a closer rein on his daughter. She raged about her standards and how I was a bad example to all the girls at our church."

"That's why I don't go to church. I know what they would say about me."

"I always felt that just by my presence, I was a constant source of embarrassment for my father. Dad made me feel like I was unstable, and just when I would start to feel acceptable as a person, someone would come along and point out my flaws."

"Religion is for good people and the rest of us just may as well hang it up 'cause we ain't going to get no better." Corette set the bundle of laundry atop the bed where Sydney had slept.

"But never to my face. They always 'reported' it to my father."

"Some people don't have enough business of they own to tend to, I guess."

"Daddy had this funny way of cringing whenever someone was putting the screws to one of us. I still flinch whenever I'm criticized."

"After you've had some breakfast with these kids, you can start by cleaning the room next to you. You need me to sit with little girl, here, you just let me know. Besides, that room, it won't be too much to clean. That customer, he never stays long. Gone before dawn, he is. Real skittish and neat."

"I never do this, Corette. You just got my life story in a bottle."

"You been needin' to talk, is all. But your baby girl, she needs tending to. Later on, after your chores tomorrow, you can take my car if you want. Get this baby to a doctor."

"I'll have to job hunt next week, I guess. If Dad could see me now, I know just what he'd say. He'd be sitting behind this big intimidating desk looking all high-and-mighty while he made me feel small and stupid."

"Your folks have a nice place, I guess."

"With a pool. He's sitting next to it right now, reading his paper and having his coffee. In the morning, he'll sit by it with a glass of juice. My mom squeezes it fresh from their own trees."

"Girl, you need to go home."

"I can't, Corette. Not like this. Sydney Oliver has to make a comeback. I can't let Wade Jenkins find me groveling like this."

"Your father, I'll bet he's seen his hard days too."

"Dad's always on top of his problems, Corette. You'll never find my father begging for his next scrap of food."

"I-I CAN'T SEE. Tell me who you are." Wade sensed several pairs of hands rifling through his pockets. A hint of perfume wafted past and he felt smaller hands yank out his wallet. He groaned when his arms were pulled behind him so that his jacket could be filched. The cold ground felt sticky against the tops of his bare feet. The rental car keys jangled and his other pocket went slack. He had been slammed against the brick wall in the alley and thrown facedown in the mud. His head throbbed from the blow of the hard tool. His bare wrist told him his watch was gone too.

Dear Lord, this can't be happening.

The assailants never spoke, although he could hear heavy breathing.

"You steal a rental car and you'll be easy to trace." He reasoned with them. His body lifted and he realized he was blindfolded. "Can I have my shoes back?" Another callous blow to his face and then all feeling left him.

13

OVERNIGHT, A FREEZE ESCAPED the gates from up north and marched into New Orleans to settle over the city. Freeze warnings sent housewives out onto their porches to bring in the ferns and let in the cat for the night. Churches, alerted to initiate the blanket and coat drives, gathered donated items into cardboard boxes for the emergency shelters.

Wade tasted blood. The smell of muddied earth had suffocated him all night. But tremors of cold moved through him. He called out for help until he felt the lull of sleep send him spiraling away from the desire to come fully awake. He couldn't breathe deeply and that affected his mind. He remembered little at first, except Isabella's face, and held on to the thread of hope that somehow she knew to pray for him. If she did, then that would account for his making it through the frigid night in an alley. Nothing else made sense. Everything else—Sydney, the kids, the thugs—all circulated in and out through the doors of his jumbled mind, fragmented, sticking to his thoughts but shredded and never congealing to form a whole, consistent body of thought.

Crumpled in what might have looked to passersby beyond the alley as a sort of dispossessed fetal slump, his chest felt kicked in. Around his rib cage, his muscles ached. So he moved his hand in a slow search up and down his right side. He wouldn't have known if it was broken or not.

The memory of being lifted and dragged and then dumped in the alley skittered through his thoughts, but he didn't trust himself to interpret the truth. The stench of whiskey assaulted his senses. Pedestrians—tourists, some of them—trekked back and forth on the sidewalk just a few yards from him. But as he leaned forward to call out again, he heard only a groan that came from deep inside him. A child glanced at him but then grabbed her mother's coattail. The sight of him must have horrified her. He ducked his head until the little girl passed by. He ached to see Isabella.

Wade dragged himself inches at a time and then propped himself up against the wall. He used the blindfold to try and clean the mud from his wounds. Someone had thrown an old blanket over him. He doubted the muggers had given it to him. Beat a man, rob him of everything he owns, and then tuck him in for the night. Not likely.

A church van backed into the alley. A nicely dressed man stepped from the passenger's side. Three others, church volunteers, followed him, calling him Pastor.

"Sir . . . Pastor, if you could—" Wade called out, weak, but stopped when he saw the cold stare of the minister.

"You'll have to take your business across town, inside the shelter, mister, just like the others," the minister said. "We only have so many coats. The mission director will check you out one, I'm sure. We're just here to pick these up."

"I'm a minister, like you. Please . . ."

"Then you're without excuse." The minister turned his back on Wade. He muttered to the others about the pathetic lengths some would go to for a handout.

"You up finally, I see."

Wade glanced up. A black man stood over him. The tatters in his coat and trousers and the bottle of gin he cradled in the crook of one arm revealed the man's dispossessed state. "I need help." He cringed. His ankle throbbed.

"I'm Charles Frances. I'm your Christmas angel."

Wade tossed aside the bandanna. The homeless man came into focus.

"You were sleeping in the mud. I hepped you over to this drier place and gave you my blanket. You must be new. I don't believe we've met."

"Thank you for the blanket, Mr. Frances. I was robbed. They stole everything. Even took my car."

"You sure about that? 'Cause I found you drunk out of your mind last night. I thought you was locked out of the shelter. If you don't get over there before nine-thirty, they lock you out, like I got locked out last night."

Wade smelled his shirt. It was he who smelled of whiskey. "They doused me with whiskey."

"Waste of the good stuff."

"Can you help me stand up, Mr. Frances? I feel kind of weak in the knees." He shuddered.

Charles Frances slid the gin into his pocket and offered Wade his hand. "You must be from out of town. I'll bet you wandered out into the cemetery. Anybody takes a walk through that cemetery might as well say bye-bye to his wallet."

"Somebody gave me bum directions. That's what I get for helping a stranger."

"Ain't too many Good Samaritans around here, sir. You best look out for yourself in this place. Lots of evil in this city. I don't sleep outside without my charms. Miss Genevieve, up the street, I get her to bless me a few charms now and then to ward off the devil."

Wade crumpled against the man.

"You hurt bad, mister."

"My ankle. I think it's sprained." Wade grimaced.

"You tell old Charles how he can hep you, sir, and he'll try his best."

"It's so cold. I thought winter passed New Orleans by."

"We got our own kind of winter. Cold at night. Warmer by da afternoon."

"Or, first, maybe if I could find a police officer."

"I don't go around too many of those kind of people. I can hep you find a coat and some shoes if that would be to your liking."

"I could use both, Mr. Frances. Just until I can try and get some things of my own."

"I like how you call me 'Mister.' You has a fine quality about you."

"They even took my pocket change. I don't have the money to make a phone call."

"If you got family, you can reach them, I'll bet. Call collect, I always say."

"I can. But I should tell the police what happened."

"You staying near here, I guess."

"The Bourbon Wyndham. But the thugs took everything, my credit cards, ID, and even my shoes. My luggage with all of my clothes was in the trunk. They even took my rental car." His feet tingled.

"Coat first, then. They got good shoes coming in nowadays down at the mission. Say you picked yourself a fine hotel. I stayed near the Bourbon once."

NONE OF THE CLINICS had an opening for Allie. Each receptionist asked Sydney for a referral, for her insurance policy, anything that would guarantee payment.

"You just pick yourself a clinic and take that little girl in and axe them what they going to do about it. They can't turn you away," said Corette.

"If I have to do that, I will. Surely some clinic will bill me."

"Now dat is a problem when you don't have yourself a permanent address."

Sydney dressed Allie in tights. The weather had turned mean.

"You can't take her out without a coat neither. Girl, you need a mama, dat's what."

"You know where to find a good coat, cheap, I guess."

"I got me a good idea."

WADE HAD TO LEAN against Charles. It was the only way he could walk with his ankle sprained. Around his rib cage was bruised. A man in a dark suit just like one he had back home stepped out of Wade's way, the man's gaze disparaging him, sizing him up. He wanted to yell after the man that he was just like him, an honest Joe, a contributor to society. Charles paid their way onto the trolley. Wade limped to the back. The soles of his feet were tender.

"Let's take these two seats back here, then. Excuse me, ma'am." Charles navigated his way around the feet of two older women.

Wade winced when he took his seat. "Thank you, Charles. You paid my way. Isabella will never believe any of this."

"She must be your lady."

"Wonderful wife of twenty-seven years. Thinks I'm safe and sound. I've got to get back to the hotel and get squared away so I can call her."

"So what is it again that you do?"

"Pastor of a large church in Florida. I'm here on business."

"Your business done took a different road, looks like."

"Looks like we're on Basin Street." Wade nodded at a woman who was staring at him. She looked away.

"You'll like the mission pastor, Pastor Fields. He a nice man."

"I won't be staying long, Charles. Once I coordinate my staff, I'll have a car again, some decent clothes. My phone back. I just need to borrow a few things from the mission. I'll see the pastor is recompensed."

"He won't be needin' none of that business."

"That means I'll see he's paid well for helping me."

"Pastor Fields, he don't need no money. They give all their stuff away."

Wade extended another smile to the staring woman.

"Keep to yourself or I'll call the police!" The lady inched away from Wade.

"This is all an interesting education, that's all. God allows things like this to teach us lessons." Wade felt his pride ebb from him. He wanted to give that woman a thought or two of his own.

"Maybe you shouldn't talk to folks until after you find yourself presentable again." Charles averted his eyes from the irate woman.

"He wants me to see the world from a poor man's eyes. I can understand it. Although I've been poor. Bible school was no picnic, I'll tell you. Isabella and I lived in this tiny campus trailer. They didn't have couples' apartments, just these old warhorse-type trailers with bad plumbing. Sunday morning was always a surprise, finding out whether or not we'd have hot water to shower for church. And that first tiny trailer we lived in when Sydney was just a newborn, why we had to keep her crib in our bedroom."

"We on Loyola now. The mission isn't far."

"This blanket smells like dirty socks. Charles, I'll buy you a new blanket if you'll throw this one away."

"Maybe Pastor Fields, he can get you a doctor."

"I don't need a doctor. Just a shower and a change of clothes. Sydney never liked our parsonage in Tennessee either. Said it made her feel as though she were 'visiting' her own home. I never understood what she meant by that."

"That there's St. John the Baptist. They got a nice school for kids. I always said if I had kids, I'd want them to go to a place like that."

"My head is killing me. I hope your pastor has some painkillers."

"If the doctor's in today, he'll hep you out with your headache. Down there's the Blue Moon. They got candy and beer. 'Course you probably don't need none of that. Gator's Discount have lots of stuff. Maybe you can buy you some clothes in there."

"Here I am rambling about myself. Charles, you must have family somewhere around Louisiana."

"Not too many of my folks left. Here's the mission. We need to get off here at Oretha Haley. Excuse, ladies."

Wade meandered around feet that pulled away in fear before he stepped out into the sunshine. The morning had a chill to it, but the day held a promise of warmth. "After you, Charles."

"Best hurry, Preacher. Folks is staring at you."

14

THE NEW ORLEANS MISSION had a displaced aura about it, like a little boy's shoe box filled with broken jacks and twigs and rubber bands so old they would not stretch but would only break, as everything in the box was broken. The mission was decorated in that hit-and-miss fashion, with donated chairs and plaques and pictures that blessed Jesus all filling the room in a practical manner but yet, to Wade, still holding an emptiness about it. And yet, the men who worked to fill the mission with life had a glimmer about them, as though they hoped. But they carried their hope around for a hundred others who had laid it aside years ago. Hope weighed heavily on those few shoulders.

Charles seated Wade in the dayroom and then, in a dutiful fashion, placed his own dirt-stained knapsack in one of the cages provided for the men's belongings. A television flashed scenes of a woman who won the jackpot on a quiz show. The sound was muted even though three men sat in front of the television and stared. Wade could see an alleyway through the window where two men conversed and smoked.

A soda clattered down through a drink machine and out into the waiting hands of a man whose coat was a size too big. It made Wade feel thirsty and desperate for pocket change. Suddenly self-conscious about his own bare feet, he crossed his ankles in an attempt to try and hide them. He sensed a pair of eyes bearing down on him. One of the television vigilantes had turned around in his chair and stared at Wade's feet, too, as well as his black eye.

"You must have tied one on last night," the man said.

Wade didn't answer.

"Suit yourself. Won't make no friends like that."

All at once, the doors beyond the dayroom opened. More indigent men and a few women gathered in the lobby and talked. A black man led two other men who carried boxes. "Donny, put those right there. All of you form a line, please."

At once the men and women gathered all around the boxes.

"Hurry, Preacher. We got coats here today," Charles said. He held a place in line for Wade.

His head throbbed even worse. Once he had shoes on his feet, he planned to spring out of the mission and head straight for the hotel. But as he took his place behind Charles, the mission pastor asked for his identification.

"You ever been here before, sir?"

"Pastor Fields, this here is a preacher, too, just like you." Charles stepped aside to give Fields a full view of Wade.

"You're a preacher." The pastor stepped toward Wade. He sniffed the air. "This man's drunk, Charles. You know the rules."

"No, Pastor. This man is dry as they come. He came to town, a visitor to our fine city, and got knocked in the head up at St. Louis Number One. They took his coat, his wallet, his shoes, and even his rental car."

"No one goes into St. Louis Number One."

"I was misguided."

"You filed a police report, sir?" Fields stared down at Wade's feet.

"Not yet. I need a coat and some shoes. Charles was kind enough to, that is, I'm Pastor Wade Jenkins. He held out his hand. If you'll just call Clearwater Freewill Tabernacle, talk to Carol Beaman—she's my secretary. She'll take care of helping me out with my personal belongings. And if I could have a word with her—"

"I'm sorry. I can help you out with a coat and some shoes at least. You got a place to stay?"

"The Bourbon New Orleans Wyndham."

"I'll drive you there myself, Pastor Jenkins. I'm sorry you've met up with some of our less than hospitable citizens."

"Hey, where's the party?" A woman pushed her way to the front of the line. "Ladies first, gentlemen."

"Corette, you know you have to get at the end of the line just like everyone else," said Fields.

"I'm on a mission of mercy. I need a coat for a little girl." Corette had an S-shaped posture and stood with her hips jutted forward, legs apart. Her nails were painted a bright pink and decorated with tiny white daisies.

"Sounds like a new angle. This is for her yard sale, I'll bet."
Charles said it in warning to Pastor Fields.

"Corette, you don't have a little girl," said Fields.

"It's for a friend in need. I'm helping out the needy. What's
wrong with that?"

"You still got to take your place at the end of the line."

Corette disappeared behind the men.

"Donny, you take care of the coat distribution. I'll be gone for
about fifteen minutes. You can follow me, sir." Fields led Wade
through a door. "We have some shoes back here. You lost your
socks, too, I guess."

"They were caked with mud. I don't remember a lot about last
night. I spotted my socks in the mud this morning when Charles
found me."

"If this is a wild story, it's the wildest I ever heard. But those
cemeteries, they're the worst place for tourists to go. You can't go
to St. Louis Number One in the daytime, let alone at night. They
say that one's haunted. You ever heard of Marie Laveau?"

Wade rummaged through a cardboard box. He was relieved
to find a pair of brown socks. "Marie Laveau. Sounds familiar."

"She was the famous Voodoo Queen of New Orleans. She's
buried in Number One. Her followers still visit her grave site."

"Good, these are my size. Thank you, Pastor Fields."

"Not that I believe in ghosts."

"Me neither. You say you got some shoes?"

"This way."

"I preached once in a mission. I should say I practiced on them—
it was homework. The men weren't allowed to eat until I'd said the
final 'amen.' Sort of a captive audience."

Pastor Fields fixed him up with a pair of sneakers that nearly fit. "Now, let's try and find you a coat out there before they're all gone. That Corette is a bad one to take more than what she needs for her yard sales."

"She's a character, I gather."

"Corette's a lady of the night. We got lots of those around here. But she stays at her own place, some dive called the Budget Palace. She only comes around when we have a coat drive."

Wade had tired of chatting. He wanted to file the police report and climb between the clean sheets of the hotel bed and nap for an hour. He followed Nivan Fields around the group of those waiting for coats, past the prostitute with the pink cast to her hair, and away from the mission. It made no sense to him why he had ended up so far from his journey to find Sydney. He was glad to leave this place behind and get on track again with his own mission.

"IT'S NOT FANCY, and a little big on her, but she'll stay warm. Got one for the little boy too." Corette held up a corduroy parka. She held it out in a ginger fashion, as though she didn't know how to give something away.

"Thanks, Corette. Trevor, thank Corette for the coat."

"It smells like cigarettes," said Trevor.

"I guess I'll go then. You got my car keys. What time you think you'll be back?"

"Maybe in a couple of hours. I don't know how long it will take, especially since they'll have to squeeze us in." Sydney watched her go. Corette had an old Monte Carlo, electric blue with a sound system that thundered. The damp air caused Allie to cough even more.

Trevor shivered as she let him into the backseat.

"I know it's cold. But we need to be thankful for a warm car and these coats."

"Thank you, God, for the warm car and the stinky coat," said Trevor.

Sydney laughed. It occurred to her that God laughed too.

15

THE SNEAKERS, too big for Wade's size-ten feet, weighed against his ankles like wobbling anchors. The Wyndham clerk stared him up and down but never looked Wade in the eye when he answered. As a matter of fact, he mostly answered Pastor Fields, who spent more time than was necessary explaining Wade's dilemma as though Wade were mute and could not speak for himself.

The clerk, whose name tag said only Armand, nodded in slight fluttering acknowledgments. He paused in brief interludes of silence to allow his eyes to trace a straight line from Fields to Wade and then straight down to Wade's muddy trousers.

"Has he any identification, Pastor Fields?"

"No, and you can ask me directly. I can speak for myself. As Pastor Fields explained, here is a copy of the police report. I need to check into my room at once. I need access to a phone and a quiet room—and I mean really quiet. The rental car agent should know the car was stolen. I have to arrange some money to be wired by my secretary—"

"We have a quiet office, Pastor Fields, where you can conduct your business with us and this man. If we provide our office to you all, do you think you could assist your Mr. Jenkins into it?" The clerk whispered to Fields.

"Assist me? I can walk on my own two feet! I'm no derelict! And the only room I want is the one reserved in my name."

"Armand, what is the problem?" A manager arrived. He appeared to be from India but spoke decent English.

"Pastor Fields from the mission, sir. He's brought this man in claiming he is a client from Florida who never checked in—a Pastor Wade Jenkins."

"Who is Pastor Jenkins?"

"I'm Jenkins."

"Your wife has been calling, Pastor Jenkins. Have you had an accident?"

"Yes, a slight one. All of my belongings were stolen."

"Pastor Jenkins, I am the manager, Hasin. Armand, this man has met with enough complications. Let's not add any more. Pastor Jenkins, if you will follow me, I shall have one of our people connect you with your family in Florida. If one of them will simply verify your identity to me over the phone, we will assist you to your room. After you've rested, I'll call our shuttle driver and he will take you wherever you need to go. Shopping first, perhaps? I can recommend a good men's store to you."

"I have the police report."

"Not necessary. Just a call to your wife, perhaps. We have her number."

⁓

ISABELLA'S VOICE sounded sweet to Wade, like nectar.

"I've been worried sick, Wade! I called the hotel this morning and they told me you never checked in. Imagine how frazzled everyone is. And Carol, well, Carol's near to calling out the National Guard."

"Isabella, I need for you to listen to me. Have some money wired to the First National Bank here at . . . hold on." Wade handed the phone to Hasin and allowed him to give her the address. Hasin had to say the address three times and finally spelled out the street name to Isabella. Wade took back the phone. "I need enough cash to buy some clothes. I was robbed, honey. Don't overreact. . . . It was in the cemetery. . . . I know. You told me. . . . No, you don't need to come here. Listen to me, honey. I'll need enough cash for some clothes and a piece of luggage and some toiletries. Call our credit card company and put a stop to charges right away. . . . I know it's Christmas, honey. Have them send you a replacement. . . . You have to listen to me, Isabella."

"We can provide your toiletries, Pastor Jenkins," Hasin interjected.

"I'll bet you're near starvation, Wade. This is all my fault. I made you feel guilty. Or else you would still be safe at home." Isabella sounded distraught on her end of the phone.

"Don't worry about food, Isabella. I'll charge my meals to the room." She always got off on her guilt trips.

"Carol can take care of the hotel bill." Isabella sniffed.

"Sounds good. Now I need to know if you've heard anything from Sydney. We have to keep our focus, Isabella. Let's get our girl and the grandkids back home. Everything else can take care of itself."

"You want Sydney to come home, Wade?"

"More than anything."

"I have her room ready. I even put up her old Christmas tree from her dorm."

"That's nice."

"You'll call me, then, later today? I hate sitting around worrying. I'm nearly sick about all of this. Did those men hurt you? I hope you had them arrested."

"I'm fine. Just some thugs. They knocked me around but got away. The cops say it's a ring that targets tourists. I helped some nice lady with a ride home and it turns out she's not so nice, they think. They called her Millie the Mugger, or some such. But a Christmas angel rescued me."

"An angel. You saw one. Evelyn Gordon thinks her missionary son is the only man alive who's seen a real one. I'll have to tell her he's not the only one receiving omissions from God."

"Emissaries. No, you won't tell anyone. I'll tell you all about it when I get home. I have to get to my room. You wouldn't believe me now if you saw me. The hotel clerk took me for a homeless guy. Imagine."

"Don't buy a yellow shirt. You know how sallow it makes you look."

"I love you."

"I love you, Wade. I want you home."

"Soon, Isabella. Pray I find Sydney today."

"We're all praying. You know that."

"I do."

◯◯

"ALLIE, LEAVE THAT DOLL in the car. It's not, well, presentable, honey." They already looked like refugees. Sydney had borrowed an outfit from Corette, black knit pants with an oversized red sweater for warmth. Crocheted roses decorated the sweater's worn yoke. She parked the electric blue Monte Carlo at the rear of the clinic. The less attention she drew to her situation, the better.

"I want my doll, Mommy. She's full of candy."

"It's okay to pretend, but let's do it later. Please don't take her inside. We can find a book to read inside the clinic."

"I'm not pretending. She's full of candy. See her foot? Peek in and see."

Sydney pushed a finger into the hole on the doll's leg. "This doll's stuffed with plastic. Allie, this is a cheap doll. We should throw it away."

"No, candy, Mommy."

Sydney set Allie back on the rear car seat. She pulled out some more seams. A plastic packet fell onto Allie's lap, clear plastic with a white powdery substance inside. Sydney felt faint. "You didn't eat any of the candy, did you, Allie? Tell Mommy you didn't!"

"You're yelling," said Allie.

Sydney picked up the packet and stuffed it back into the leg. "This can hurt you, Allie! Tell me you didn't eat it."

Allie started to cry. "I didn't!"

127

A patrol car pulled into the parking lot, drove past them, then circled back out again. Sydney kept her back to the policeman and pretended to fiddle with Allie's seat belt. She felt rage. "This is a bad doll. You say Daddy had this doll in his gun case?"

Allie nodded. Tears formed at the corners of her eyes. "Am I bad too?"

"You should never take something without asking. Haven't I told you that?" She held Allie close. "Don't cry. You're not bad." Sydney spotted a waste receptacle. But if the cop or someone else saw her stuff it in, if the doll showed up somewhere unexpected or fell into the wrong hands, she could be tied in with it. Or some kid might find it. Her pulse skipped a beat. If she handed it over to the police, they would interrogate her, grill the kids. Ray could be implicated. The kids would see their father taken off to jail. She had to take the doll back to Pierre. He knew the ins and outs of this underworld business, could identify the white powder. He would know what to do.

"Allie, let's hide the dolly in the trunk. After you see the doctor, we'll figure out how to get rid of it."

AFTER WADE dressed himself in a terry hotel robe, he gave his clothes to the bellhop and asked him to have them cleaned. Attached was a note signed by Hasin that instructed that Pastor Jenkins's laundry be cleaned immediately and returned to him at once.

He locked the door behind the bellhop, finished off the two chocolates left on his pillow, and ordered a large steak and a potato from room service. The bedroom was furnished in what looked to be fashionable antiques and all sorts of elegant finishing touches that would have sent Isabella all around the room snapping photos to take home and add to her decorating catalogs. The only thing that mattered to him were the clean linens.

He ignored the flashing telephone signal, knowing it was only the customary welcome from the hotel management. He headed for the bathroom. The shower cleansed away the alley mud and dried blood from his limbs and face. Hot steam billowed around him and clouded the glass shower door. Twice he lathered himself with the hotel soaps, feeling more validated as a man with each washing. His head dropped forward with his hands pressed against the porcelain lining. A groaning sigh emanated from him as the water streamed over his neck and down his back.

After the shower, he wrapped himself in the robe again and sat near the large plate-glass window that overlooked the canal to wait for his meal and clean clothes. Sleet spattered against the glass, tiny razor pebbles that flew at him and then pelted to the street below to melt into the gutters. Residents of the fashionable flats had outlined their windows, some with white Christmas lights and others with the traditional Mardi Gras colors of purple, gold, and green. The wintry mix of rain and sleet shimmered in sullied outlines along rooftops and passing automobiles, blending with the garish lights of New Orleans and the frill of blinking Christmas accoutrements. No noon-day sun broke through, only the tactile gray blanket of clouds that turned the day to night and the city into a brash village of blaring horns and hungry lunch-hour pedestrians.

A clutter of papers lay near the phone where the bellhop had cleaned out what few items remained in Wade's pockets. He plucked a folded note from the nightstand and opened it. It read:

Reverend Hank DeLucey, International Outreach Community Church.
In his haste with Isabella, he had forgotten to ask her if Carol had
found out anything else about DeLucey or why Trevor would have
access to his cellular phone. He reached for the phone and dialed
the church's number.

"Yes, I'm Pastor Wade Jenkins from Clearwater Freewill in
Tampa Bay. I'd like to have a word with Pastor DeLucey. . . . No,
I don't have an appointment. But this is an urgent matter. . . . I
should make an appointment? All right, then. I'd like to meet with
Pastor DeLucey later this afternoon. No, next week won't work."
He stood to allow the room service attendant inside to set up for his
meal. "I'm quite aware that we're in the middle of the holiday
season. As I said, it's urgent. . . . No, I can't meet with an associate
pastor. It's paramount that I meet with DeLucey. . . . I do understand how important Reverend DeLucey is." Wade rolled his eyes
and waited. He overheard a conversation between the secretary
and another person.

She apologized and told him that Reverend DeLucey had no
openings until sometime the end of January.

"Is Reverend DeLucey standing nearby?"

He heard a silent pause.

"If he is, please give him this message: I have his cell-phone
number and I'll continue to call him on it until he agrees to see me."
Wade rattled off the cell number given to him by Carol. "How did I
get his private cell number? I'd rather explain that to Pastor DeLucey
in person, if that's all right with you."

He overheard whispering.

The secretary said, "Reverend DeLucey can see you this afternoon at three-thirty, but only for ten minutes."

"You're a peach. Now I need directions from the Wyndham New Orleans. Yes, it's a very nice hotel. I agree, the antiques here are quite tasteful." Wade scribbled down the directions from the secretary. He had three hours to make himself presentable. "Good day to you, too, ma'am."

The food arrived. He added a tip to the ticket and dismissed the bellman.

The sleet pelted the glass even harder as the clouds spread into a solid mass of iron gray. A homeless woman wrapped in a thin shawl that waved behind her pushed a rickety cart up the street. Wade wondered if she knew that it was coat day at the mission. He bowed and said a silent prayer for Sydney and the kids. He felt a little unsettled about it, but that was natural.

16

WADE ESTIMATED that International Outreach Community Church was twice the size of Clearwater Freewill. The secretarial pool alone filled three large rooms, the last of which served only Pastor Hank DeLucey. The hotel shuttle driver had told him that six months ago the church had fired up a broadcasting ministry, aiming its sights toward syndication—all the brainchild of DeLucey, a small-town preacher who had grown a large congregation on charisma and a southern-fried preaching ability. Over the last few weeks, the show had been syndicated in twenty-seven cities. Wade studied the portrait of DeLucey and his wife, DeLynn. He entertained himself with a silent game—he linked DeLucey's wife's first name with her surname, then reversed them, then invented a limerick. *DeLynn was the wife of DeLucey. . . .*

"Pastor Jenkins, Reverend DeLucey will see you now."

He took a few steps toward the receptionist and saw how she studied his face. In order to keep her attention away from the oversized sneakers, he extended his hand and offered a greeting a little too overcharged with sentiment. He caught his own reflection in an ornate lobby mirror and realized the ridiculous overture did not suit him. Even though he had had his clothing restored to him, he felt less than presentable. The hotel dry cleaners had returned the articles in just enough time for him to head for International Outreach. The jacket and clothing had cleaned up presentably enough, but once he stepped onto the curb of the church, he noticed a faded smear on one shirtsleeve. The church was warm inside, but he would have to keep hold of his coat. The cheap mission socks chafed his injured ankles. Tonight, if he felt he had sufficient leads to Sydney and the kids, he would make time to forage through the men's department stores.

"You must have had a really bad accident," she said. The secretary studied the bruise around his cheek and eye.

"I was mugged."

"First time to New Orleans?"

"Interesting Welcome Wagon you all offer here."

"They say crime has decreased here. Guess they couldn't prove it by you." Her nervous laugh annoyed Wade. "Can I get you coffee or a Coke?"

"A cola would be nice. I need to take a couple of aspirin."

She disappeared. Another secretary propped open the office door with her foot while she invited Wade toward her with a quick hand motion as though she were fanning a candle. "This way, Pastor Jenkins." She wore a wreath-shaped brooch with a ribbon across the girth of it that read, "Jesus is the reason for the season."

Wade passed through two more offices and counted twelve men and women all engaged in an assortment of tasks from answering the phones that rang incessantly to designing brochures on computer screens. Piped-in music featured a gospel quartet that sang of old time religion and brush arbors and river baptisms.

A college student who spoke on the phone wound up a toy monkey and released it. His eyes followed the tin toy as it clanked across his desktop, banging a yellow drum.

The secretary Wade followed pressed an intercom button next to a large oak door. "Reverend Jenkins is here to you see you, sir."

"Send him in."

She opened the door for Wade and then closed it behind him. DeLucey sat behind a heavy desk. Behind him were bookcases lined with immaculate books that Wade estimated had never been opened.

"Pastor Jenkins, welcome to International Outreach," DeLucey said. He spoke with a rigid jaw and enunciated his words in a way that made all of his vowels sound round, as though the inside of his mouth shaped every word with a resonate O. He rose from his chair only halfway and extended his hand. Several gold rings decked his fingers.

"Nice setup." Wade shook his hand and then took a seat across from DeLucey.

"Started out in a small barn with dirt floors. God blessed our little flock."

"To say the least."

"This here picture's of my son, Hank Jr., and his wife, Delilah.

These are my grandkids." DeLucey's wrist pivoted out from the center of his chest and then pointed toward the credenza full of photos.

"They'll steal your heart," said Wade. "You'll go to the ends of the earth to see they're all right. I guess you understand that."

"Mister, er, Pastor Jenkins, I know you mentioned to Sal that you're here on urgent business. If this has something to do with my cell phone, well, it's been missing for several days."

Wade felt himself deflate.

"I don't remember exactly where I laid it down, but I'd sure like to have it back if you've come across it."

"I don't know where it is, Reverend DeLucey. Only that my missing grandson made a call to my church from it."

"Your grandson is missing? How tragic."

"He's with his mother and his sister. But they're on the run from an abusive situation."

DeLucey's eyes stared in an oblique line to his left. "You've called the police."

"I discussed it with the local police just this morning when I filed the report about my mugging." Wade told him everything, including Ray's lie about Sydney's staying with a friend.

"You were mugged and you have missing family members. I'd say God is trying to get your attention, Pastor Jenkins."

Wade held his words.

"So, the police, I assume they are the ones that traced the number to your grandson."

"No, it was my secretary. We reported Sydney's disappearance to the police, but they think my daughter's situation is simply a family quarrel. Her husband played the abandoned spouse and worried father when they called him. If I can find some proof that she's in danger, well, I have to find her and the kids or at least figure out where they've been. I've tried to reason with her husband, but he insists she left the home angry, and he won't tell me where she is. I was hoping you might give me an idea of where you think you left your phone."

"As a pastor I'm sure you know I visit all sorts of neighborhoods. I was hopeful that a church member would phone and tell me that I had left it behind in their home."

"You visit your own church members?"

"Mostly, my associate pastors take care of visits. But I make a few calls from time to time. It's how I keep my hand on the pulse of the people."

"So you don't recall being anywhere around a mother and two little ones, little dark-haired boy and girl. Big brown eyes. Cute kids, both of them. Pretty like their mother. Sydney comes to about here when I'm standing up." He made a knifing motion just below his shoulder. "Reddish brown, straight hair. Hangs around her shoulders."

"I see families like that all the time."

"I suspect my little granddaughter might even be sick."

"Here's what you do. You stop by and see Sal—she's the gal who showed you in. We have prayer partners all across the state that pray for International Outreach. You fill out a prayer card, attach a ten-dollar donation, and give it to Sal and see if you don't get your miracle, Pastor. God moves in amazing ways."

"If I attach a donation, that is."

DeLucey glanced down at his watch. "I'm afraid our ten minutes are up."

Wade had heard of men like DeLucey, but he had never seen the genuine article up close and in color.

"Well, I have good news. I have written a best-selling book. I call it *Finding Your Miracle*. Tell you what, I'll give you an autographed copy to read yourself, but you be sure and let everyone know when you find your miracle how God used this book to meet you at your point of need."

"Here's your cola, Pastor Jenkins." The receptionist peered in through the large doorway.

"No need. I'm leaving." *DeLucey here'll want a donation for that, too, and I'm fresh out,* he thought.

She smiled and revealed a set of braces decorated with festive red and green bands. "Have yourself a miraculous day, Pastor Jenkins. And remember, 'Jesus is the reason—'"

Wade sidled past. His ankle throbbed. "God bless."

"Pastor, you keep looking for your miracle," said DeLucey. "Don't forget to pick up your copy of . . ."

Wade stalked out to the waiting taxi. DeLucey's cell-phone number had only been another dead end. He prayed a worried prayer. Inside, he ached. Outside, his muscles were stiff and his joints tender. North seemed south. The sparse parking lot confused him until he realized he had walked out of the wrong exit. Before crossing back through the portals of DeLucy's lair, though, he would rather limp for miles. He followed the walk around the church until he saw the hotel shuttle parked beside the front entrance. The driver read a newspaper. A groan slipped from Wade's mouth when he clambered into the backseat.

"Where we going, Pastor?"

He stared out the window at the massive church that held no

answers. A tremor ran from his neck to his arms. "I don't know. Just drive."

SYDNEY PULLED the blanket up to Allie's chin. "Corette's coming over to sit with you two while I go see Pierre." Trevor's eyes closed. Sydney's quiet bustling around the motel room as she fussed over Allie lulled him to sleep.

Sydney heard a tap at the door. She opened it and found Corette rubbing her arms.

"Thank you, Corette. Her fever's better. The doctor says it's a virus. He gave us some medicine. Enough samples to see her through this."

"They's still nice people in the world. Say, I been looking for something. One of my customers left it behind, he say, and, chère! Does this fellow have a short fuse!"

"It wouldn't be here, Corette."

"You remember anyting, anyting at all, like maybe something showed up in the laundry?"

"Trevor got into the laundry and made tents with the sheets. But he's asleep."

Corette crept to his side. She lifted his covers to pull them over him. A cellular phone slid to the floor.

"Is that what you're looking for, Corette?" Sydney picked it up and handed it to her. "This would account for that chirping noise."

"Land, that man, he's so mad, he accuse me of making calls on his private phone. I take this back to him. Or at least leave it some-place where he can find it."

139

"I'm sorry, Corette."

"I know your kids. They good kids. He should watch his own tings better."

"He must be a businessman or something. That phone looks expensive."

"If I told you the truth, you'll not believe Corette, dat's what."

Sydney shoved the doll into a plastic trash bag.

"He'll be glad to see dis. Den I make sure he not leave it behind again. Dis man a good customer."

Corette opened the door for Sydney. "You look white, like you seen a ghost, chère. Go on den over to Pierre's office and he'll be waiting. I told him you said it was important."

More sleet and rain misted the walk around the motel room doorway. Sydney heard Corette bolt and lock the door behind her. Before Corette arrived, she had told Trevor, "You need to pray. Mommy needs a miracle."

Maybe it's Mommy who should pray, she thought. *If I can remember how.*

17

WADE WALKED ALONG The Riverwalk, an amalgam of shops on Poydras that reminded him of the Baltimore Inner Harbor, where he and Isabella had once taken Sydney and Lance to the National Aquarium. Shopping-intent pedestrians surged like scrambling crabs around Wade, although not in the same crushing throng in which he and Isabella had almost lost one another in Baltimore.

A high school band dressed in white uniforms festooned with bright red plumes played "O Come, All Ye Faithful" atop the tiled court of Spanish Plaza. Wade moved beyond the band to take in the view of the river. Local flotillas meandered down the Mississippi in anticipation of the Christmas bonfires that would rise up after sunset along the levees each night until Christmas Eve when all of Louisiana welcomed Papa Noel. Wade peeled off his jacket.

The world had become sunny again. Along the lapping waters of the Mississippi, three sanderlings with feathers whitened by the cool kiss of a Southern winter danced along the shoreline to dodge the pulse of muddy tide and forage for insects. There was a lapse in time, as though parts of him ebbed away from the shore, peeled from his prickling realities. He found himself in front of the shops again and could no more remember walking away from the river's view than he could remember the details of being stripped of his belongings and dignity the night before.

A store that specialized in athletic shoes caught his attention. He stopped in and bought a pair of low-end sneakers and athletic socks, glad to leave the mission shoes in a nearby waste can. An hour later, he had several bags filled with shirts, slacks, and underwear. Over his shoulder he strapped on a new duffel bag.

He stopped for coffee and beignets at Café du Monde and then made a collect call from a pay phone to Isabella, who had heard nothing from Sydney. But she said that Lance had called and would be home for Christmas with his wife and three children. She didn't know where to put them. Isabella spared Sydney's older brother the details of Wade's trip in hopes that all would be well by Christmas Day.

Wade assured Isabella he had restocked his traveling wardrobe with all of the right colors, said his I-love-you's, and then reminded her he had a daughter to locate. After he emptied the remainder of ibuprofen into his palm, he swallowed the three pills to quell the wrenching pain around his sprained ankle.

As he twisted the store bag loops onto his wrists, he heard a familiar voice. He turned to his left and almost expected to see a family he knew from Tampa Bay. He only saw the back of a woman's head as she spoke to a man on a bench. In a casual jaunt, he made an arc around the bench and cast an oblique gaze toward the woman. Her hair had changed to a curly black shag, but he knew the eyes and the mouth, the tilt of her head, and the gallingly recognizable story of a woman needing a lift to the airport. He thought about shouting out her name, exposing her collusive plot to ruin him. But he only stared at her.

Her face drew up and her eyes had a glassy cast, like a fish pulled up alongside a stern. She jumped to her feet and knocked over the other man's coffee.

Wade spotted a security guard. "You know that lady's wanted by the cops."

The security officer grew rigid. Wade lost sight of her when she ran into a crowd that had gathered to listen to the Riverwalk jazz band. The guard said, "What's the problem, sir?"

"That woman's part of some mugging operation."

"You sure it's her? Because I don't want no trouble."

Wade saw that she was getting away. Two steps away from the guard, pain spiked up his leg like darts.

"You okay, mister? You don't look so good."

"Please call the police." Wade followed her into the crowd. The bags jostled around him, wrapped around him, and pummeled him as he shoved through the shoppers.

The woman dashed through an open square and made straight for Poydras, where she disappeared into a cab.

Wade broke through to the square. The security guard had not bothered to follow him. Instead of lining up along the streets in New Orleans, cabbies wandered around until a pedestrian managed to catch the driver's attention. Wade stumbled out into the street, his eyes darting up and down the busy stretch of Poydras until he spotted the yellow cab. Millie's cab disappeared into the thrum and beat of the city.

Volumes of sunlight warmed Wade's forehead. Worry swarmed his mind, fecund thoughts that discovered a fertile hole of anxiety within a father's heart.

Sydney had not called her mother or the church since his departure from Tampa Bay. Ray Oliver had stopped answering the phone altogether. Trevor's mystery call from DeLucey's cellular phone had led Wade nowhere. And now a woman he scarcely knew had sidetracked him here in a shopping mall. Sydney would say it was the black-and-white of it all that drove him to see that the woman was brought to justice. He had a choleric need to right the wrongs and bring to light things hidden. She had said that about him once—that he was all black-and-white—and asked him if he ever saw anything in life as gray or in between. He held on to the back of a bus bench and wondered if his daughter wanted to be found by him. The thought that she didn't terrified him. The realization that he might not ever locate her made him ill. Or if he found her, he wondered if he lacked the words that would convince her to come home with him. In her last attempt to speak with him, she had been left on hold to listen to hymns of praise while she waited in line to have a turn with the big guy, the pastor of Clearwater Freewill Tabernacle. He always thought she had understood his responsibilities. Pictures of where she might be at this moment made a fearsome carousel around his thoughts. Ray Oliver had been more than just a termite in the Jenkins family. He was a threat, and Wade had ignored the problems until all of the people he cherished had vanished. Sydney, Trevor, and Allie were in danger and too alienated from him to ask for help.

He waved the bags in the air until the driver pulled up alongside him with his window cracked open.

The driver fought with the gearshift.

Wade hopped in and emptied his arms of the bags. "I need to find a gift, something nice for a young woman, my daughter."

"Price no object, sir?"

"Price no object." Wade rubbed the swollen egg-shaped bruise on his ankle.

"New Orleans Centre. That's a good place to shop if you got the income."

"She's worth it."

"I guess you from out of town."

"Florida. Watch out for that pedestrian."

Wade gathered up his bags and held on to them while the cabbie passed block after block with his radio blaring a jazzy rendition of "God Rest Ye Merry, Gentlemen."

"Here's your stop."

Wade threw open the door and dragged his bags out onto the curb at New Orleans Centre, weary of the shopping load on a wounded ankle. He paid the driver.

"Good luck wit' your shopping. Women are hard to please," the driver said.

Two squad cars blocked traffic across the street. Three cops led a handcuffed woman wearing a black wig to one of the cars. Wade recognized Millie. He turned from the scene, knowing that the strings of life now pulled him through a different forest.

Wade walked into the center. He crossed the large Lord and Taylor and found the inside entry to the mall. He rode an escalator to the top and surveyed all around, down onto the main floor and into the music and beauty care stores. The Lord and Taylor entrance drew him back inside. He wandered around, stopping to consult several clerks who finally led him to the jewelry department.

"You say she was born in September?" asked the clerk.

He gave a male sort of shrug.

"This pendant has her birthstone."

He settled on the gold chain with a sapphire heart pendant and had it wrapped. Wade made his way toward a bench where he could prop up his ankle. A children's choir assembled below near the escalator and a few yards from the long line that led to the mall Santa.

He laid his bags on the bench and recalled the events of the last few hours. Before he had departed the hotel this afternoon, his voice mail at the Wyndham Orleans was packed full of messages from various nervous staff members, including Sam Farris. Farris had called for a work order to implement the funds for the frenzied sewing crew who had less than a month to reinvent the entire Christmas pageant wardrobe. The head of the church board, Frank Hazzleby, had called twice. The board's impatience to close out the end-of-year report collided with the Christmas pageant every year, right on schedule. Carol left word that he had accumulated a list of no less than sixty requests for appointments, all persons who wanted to meet with him next week for counsel, or benevolence requests, or those who wanted to sell something to the church.

Wade said a quiet prayer for his daughter, as he had done so many times over the past few days. He prayed that he would find Sydney but, most of all, that she would exonerate him of all of his fatherly crimes. There were elements imparted to Lance and Sydney that made him proud. He had taught them both to study, to apply their minds to their work. But Sydney had slipped away from his reach, had all but levitated to the wrong kind. Her habit of linking arms with the less sacred elements of humanity had driven Wade to nag her until she fell silent.

His ankle swelled. He waited on the bench for several hours, until the sky darkened again. Another day lost.

He prayed again. None of the meetings, the board problems, or even the Christmas pageant mattered at this moment. Not even Millie the Mugger.

Stacked in a display with holiday ribbons and garland, nine televisions displayed a local afternoon newsbreak. A reporter stood outside a motel, speaking into the camera while behind her a paparazzi-style press flashed camera bulbs and held boom mikes over the heads of policemen and detectives who were escorting a female perpetrator from the motel.

Two older ladies parked their plumpish bodies directly in front of a television, curious about the late-breaking story. Wade stepped toward them to see around the women and then moved in behind them. The camera caught the whole scene and played it back. A man who attempted to flee the motel scene tried to hide his face but not before the reporters could catch his flight on film. The television station played the footage several times. The police forced a house-keeper to unlock a motel room door, the officers charged the room, and then came upon a half-dressed DeLucey and a prostitute who stood holding his coat. Wade recognized the cowering visage. DeLucey had bolted wearing only his shirt and undershorts. But the police had wrestled him to the ground. He wept openly.

"That's Hank DeLucey," he said. "I just saw him today."

"On *Southern Devotions,* that religious show with all of that gospel music. My sister watches it every morning," said one woman. "Why, she even sent him money so she could get some specially anointed prayer rag for her arthritis. I told her he was a crook!"

"Caught in the act. Now that's a fine how-do-you-do for that sweet wife of his. Every time that woman cries on TV my heart just breaks. She just has such a good heart," said the other woman.

"Hank DeLucey," said Wade. He returned to the bench to gather up his bags. Before leaving, he glanced again at the television screens. Just beyond the press melee, the lone housekeeper walked down the walk of the hotel, her arms wrapped around a laundry basket full of linens. She glanced once at the camera and then turned away. When she had opened the door for the policemen, her face had not been visible—only her hands in a close-up when she unlocked the door. Now Wade saw her straight on.

He dropped his bags and pushed between the two women. "I saw a woman—a young woman in the background. You saw her, didn't you?"

"No, I didn't see anyone else, did you, Ethel?"

"Maybe I saw the maid. Is that what you saw, Blanche?"

"Auburn hair, slender girl, right?" Wade clutched the shoulder of the woman's coat.

"Did she have auburn hair, Blanche? I was looking at that DeeLoochee fellow, actually. I'd like to ask you to let go of me, sir."

"Did either of you recognize the motel?"

"There's so many of those types of motels all up and down Airline Highway, and anyway, sir, you're scaring me and we really have to be on our way."

Wade ran into the department store. He grabbed one of the

televisions, jerked it around until it faced him, and then turned up the sound.

A nervous clerk approached him. "If you need assistance with that television, we have a better display in the back of the store."

"I'm sorry. I have to see this, miss." The television newscast replayed footage of the police officers who had escorted DeLucey from the motel. Ahead of him, a woman jerked and flailed as she tried to force the cops to unhand her. She looked as familiar to Wade as DeLucey, but the camera shot panned back to DeLucey within seconds before Wade could identify her. DeLucey hid his face while in the background a young motel maid hefted laundry across a walk, tossed a brief glance toward the police scene, and ran away. The lens focused on DeLucey from that point on with a close-up of the television minister, who pulled his coat over his face. The female reporter said, "And we're live from Gaston's Budget Palace, where Reverend Hank DeLucey, television pastor of the mega International Outreach Community Church, has just been taken in for questioning with the possible charge of engaging in illicit sex with a prostitute. Police are also searching for the proprietor of the motel, Pierre Gaston, who is wanted for questioning. It is believed that Gaston's Budget Palace was being used as the shop for a prostitution ring. Three women have already been arrested and charged with prostitution. The woman you see here is Corette Fortier—a woman, police say, who has a long criminal record of prostitution. Police inform us that the sting has been under way for several days and that finding the famous television preacher in the midst of their operation was quite a surprise."

Wade hobbled through the department store to find the closest exit back to Poydras Street.

SYDNEY YANKED the doll out of the dirty linens basket. After rummaging through the closet, she decided that any place she hid the doll would be an easy find. Pierre had turned ashen when she showed it to him, and he told her to get rid of it. "Whoever owns this stash will kill for it," he had said.

"Mommy, there's cops all over and they took Miss Corette and some man. I saw Miss Corette meet him and go in her room down by the office. They were in there a long time. Did you show them where to find her?" Trevor sounded worried.

Sydney felt tremors go through her. The police had stopped her when she crossed the lot with her load of linens and had forced her to open Corette's door. A policewoman ordered her away, but she stood for a brief moment and watched as two men manhandled Corette. Pierre had fled, run out the back before the cops could catch him. Only one cop questioned her, a big officer. He let her go but warned her not to leave town; he would be watching. Her knuckles were white as she gripped the laundry basket.

"They talked to you, Mommy. Are you going to jail?"

"I'm not, Trevor. I haven't done anything wrong." Her tone sounded weak, breathy, as though she were lying. "But I shouldn't have brought us here. This was all wrong for us."

"Mommy's on TV," said Allie.

Sydney saw her own face move across the screen and then turn from the camera as she made her way back to the room. A television crew had caught her every movement. Plainly, anyone who saw the evening news report would recognize her.

She felt Allie's forehead.

"I feel better," said Allie.

Three policemen had gathered a few yards from her door. Sydney wanted to take the kids and run. But she felt glued to the faded carpet. Her pride had kept her from asking for help from the family who loved her. She could not allow Wade Jenkins to find them like this. If she could find the strength to make one call, she could get them out of here and away from Ray and his sick problems.

Trevor had left the Bible open, open to the dog-eared page. Sydney shoved the doll beneath the bed. She saw the words: *"Who touched Me?"* She ran her fingers down the page:

Now when the woman saw that she was not hidden, she came trembling; and falling down before Him, she declared to Him in the presence of all the people the reason she had touched Him and how she was healed immediately.

"Don't cry, Mommy," said Allie.

"She's not crying," said Trevor. "She's praying."

18

SYDNEY TOSSED HER BELONGINGS into a bag while Trevor and Allie played on the bed. The Budget Palace had no lights on in any room but theirs. The television crew and the police had vanished. "We're leaving, kids. Help Mommy gather up your things."

"Corette must be famous," said Trevor. "And you're famous too, I guess."

"Corette took our play phone," said Allie.

"That wasn't a play phone, Allie. That phone belonged to someone else. Apparently that television minister." Sydney scooped her toiletries into the small overnight case.

"Like Grandpa."

"No." Sydney wiped her eyes. "Nothing like Grandpa. Grandpa's a—a good pastor." She had not admitted that until now.

"Trevor talked to Grandpa on it," said Allie.

"Talked to Grandpa on that man's phone?" Sydney glanced at Trevor. "Like a play phone. Allie means that you pretended to talk to Grandpa, right, Son?"

Trevor rolled up his pajamas and stuffed them into a small bag.

"Trevor, you didn't answer Mommy."

"I wanted to talk to him and tell him we want to go back to Florida."

"That's impossible. You can't remember the number." She kept packing.

"I know how to use a phone, just like you showed me, Mommy. I know Grandpa's number. You taught me to call Grandpa or you if anything bad ever happened."

"Please tell Mommy what you told him, Trevor."

"He didn't talk to me, just a lady who didn't talk to me either but had me push all the buttons. I know all of my numbers. I can count to a hundred. Mostly, I got Grandpa's music that he likes."

"Did you leave a message?"

"I told him that Allie had a fever and that I wanted him to come and get us. I think, anyway."

"Please tell me you didn't tell him where we are."

"I wanted him to find us. I told him about the long road with the trucks on it."

"I want you both to finish up your sandwiches. Then we're leaving."

"Those policemen talked to you a long time, Mommy."

"Yes, but they're finished now."

Allie's face lifted. Her eyes were wide and she held her hand to her ear. "Listen. Somebody's here."

"Both of you sit quietly on the bed."

"It's Grandpa!" Trevor yelled.

"Trevor, please do what Mommy asks."

The sound of gravel popped outside beneath an automobile's tires. The sun had disappeared just beyond the long row of utility poles over an hour ago, the pink glow of sunset a whisper of color taken over by the night. There was a silent moment as the headlights panned the window and then went dark.

"Grandpa brings us Christmas presents," said Allie.

Sydney wished that she had turned off the motel lights. After the police raid, her room would be the only one lit.

She stiffened as she heard the inevitable knock at the door. Her heart nearly stopped when she heard her name called out.

"Sydney! You in there?"

"It's Daddy," said Allie. She moved closer to Trevor.

"Ray, just go away!" Sydney slowly lifted the bolt chain to add another lock to the door.

"You're famous, baby! They caught your smiling face on TV. You can't hide from Ray forever."

"Mommy, he's scaring me," Trevor whispered.

Ray twisted the doorknob. "Open the door, Sydney. I need something and I think you know what it is."

Sydney ran into the bathroom. Their corner room had a window in the bathroom. She could toss their things through it and then lower Trevor and Allie to the ground.

Ray kicked at the door. Allie started crying.

"Don't hit, Mommy!" Trevor shouted. "No more!"

Sydney found the window painted shut. She jabbed at the paint seal with an old car key.

"Allie, you in there, baby?" Ray spoke more softly through the door to the little girl. "You left your crayons in Daddy's gun box, baby. You found that dolly, didn't you, baby?"

"It's mine," said Allie.

"I need that dolly, Cricket. It belongs to this man out here and—"

Sydney heard a thud and then a groan. She realized Ray had brought company.

Trevor grabbed his sister's hand before she could slide to the floor and open the door. "No, Allie!"

"But he'll spank me." Allie's bottom lip quivered.

"I won't let him. Let's take our stuff to Mommy."

Before Trevor could help Allie off the bed, Ray slammed against the door. The wood splintered around the frame. He hit it again, and the door flew open.

"Sydney, you come on out of there now! Trevor, you take your little sister to the car, now, Son! Daddy and Mommy need to have a little talk."

Behind Ray, a thin man held Ray's arm behind his back.

"He's a bad man!" Trevor pushed Allie behind him.

"Do what I tell you, Son!"

Trevor grabbed Allie's hand and ran out into the dark. The two of them hurried past their father's car and across the gravel lot.

Ray leaned against the doorframe facing. The drug dealer held a gun on him.

"You just cooperate with this man, Sydney, and I swear he'll let us go." Sweat trickled down Ray's bruised head.

"He won't let us go, Ray!"

"Get the doll!" said the dealer.

Sydney's fingers curled at her sides. She held to something invisible —something bigger than Ray or the thug.

WADE FELT as though the cab moved through space in slow motion. The cabdriver had glanced at him several times in the rearview mirror to ask him if he really wanted to go to Gaston's Budget Palace. Wade held the directions in his hand.

The cab careened down Airline Highway past other motels and mom-and-pop restaurants, all of them lit up with strings of colored lights wrapped with garland in the clouded windows. Wade clasped his hands and pulled them up to his chin. He closed his eyes and relived the scene. The sight of his intelligent daughter working as a chore girl and possibly for a pimp had taken his breath from him. He knew that Trevor and Allie were there as well and tried to imagine his grandkids' faces as they witnessed the police raid. When his eyes finally met with Sydney's, she would expect him to condemn her. If he had to approach her on his knees, then so be it, he decided.

The cab slowed to pull into the motel parking lot. As the taxi turned right into the lot, the light hit two moving figures.

"What was that?" Wade sat forward.

"Looks like two kids. Small, like my own two." The Latino driver reached for a flashlight. He shined it out onto the lot but found no more movement. "You saw it too, right, mister?"

"I did." Wade threw open the door. "Please, wait here."

Every room and even the motel office looked stark and empty in the moonlight—lightless and evacuated in the night. Down at the far end, a light shone from an open motel room door. He walked toward it. Out front was parked an old car. Wade knew that it wasn't the car that he and Isabella had bought for Sydney. A child's voice, like that of a little girl crying, drew Wade away from the doorway. He followed it across the lot and behind the motel office.

◦─◦

SYDNEY LAY CRUMPLED on the bathroom floor. When she had tried to run past Ray, he had grabbed her and shoved her to the floor. When she fell, she had hit her lip against the lavatory sink. She touched her lip and drew back blood. "Is this the way we end, Ray?"

"Give him the doll, Sydney! Can't you see he's going to kill me?"

"You care so little about our kids. . . . You dragged us into this mess."

"I did it for us. Nothing I did was good enough for you. You think I don't care, but I do."

"You've never cared about us."

"Don't tell me what I care about. You think you're better than me. You and your family. Ray Oliver cares, and that's what our kids are going to know. Now get up and go find that doll!"

"Shut up!" said the dealer.

"Drop it!"

Ray's chest heaved as he glanced to his left. The dealer stiffened as the cop pressed his pistol into the back of his head.

"Pierre!" Sydney saw the motel clerk standing behind the cop. Behind him stood her father. "Daddy!" She ran to him. *Dear Jesus,* she thought. *You heard me.* She sobbed as she pressed her face against her father's chest.

Wade bent down and cradled his daughter in his arms while Trevor and Allie clung to his jacket. "I called Pierre, here, after seeing the news report. He heard my voice on the motel answering machine and decided to help out. He told me how to get here. He saw the dealer come into the room. He risked his own arrest to call the police, Sydney."

"Pierre, thank you so much."

Pierre stood with his hands in his pockets. He offered the cop a weak smile.

Trevor crawled under the bed and pulled out the doll. He handed it to the cop.

Ray glared at Sydney. "It's over between us, Sydney!"

She kissed her father's face. "I know, Ray. Daddy, let's go home."

19

SYDNEY HEARD the jangle of tin bells outside the room where she had once slept.

"We're about to hang the jingle-bell wreath on the door, Sydney. It's tradition," said Isabella.

"I'll be out in a minute, Mother." Sydney waited for her mother to jingle down the hallway to join Trevor and Sydney in a decorating frenzy. Isabella had dug out all of Sydney's old dorm decorations and left them in the guest room: a tabletop Christmas tree, plastic tree lights shaped like snowmen, a collection of Christmas bears, and a surplus of mismatched candleholders with the old candles still intact. She lit each one and placed them in a semicircle around the tree next to the bed.

Her Bible from college lay next to a gold band, a ring given to

Sydney her freshman year by her mother. Sydney slid it on the finger where she had once worn Ray's department-store wedding band. The Bible had no conspicuous bookmarks placed inside of it—an old habit of her mother's, deployed whenever she was trying to drive home a point. It was simply there on the table with Sydney's name inscribed upon it. She sat on the bed, opened the cover, and listened to the sound of her own breathing. The story trickled back to her.

The inspirational Christmas music that played in the living room changed songs twice before Sydney found the story that caught her eye back at the Budget Palace. She read it again, but unhurriedly:

And there was a woman in the crowd who had had a hemorrhage for twelve years. She had spent everything she had on doctors and still could find no cure. She came up behind Jesus and touched the fringe of his robe. Immediately, the bleeding stopped.

"Who touched me?" Jesus asked.

Everyone denied it, and Peter said, "Master, this whole crowd is pressing up against you."

But Jesus told him, "No, someone deliberately touched me, for I felt healing power go out from me." When the woman realized that Jesus knew, she began to tremble and fell to her knees before him. The whole crowd heard her explain why she had touched him and that she had been immediately healed. "Daughter," he said to her, "your faith has made you well. Go in peace."

TREVOR SANG "SILENT NIGHT" for his grandparents. Sydney heard it and imagined him standing ceremonially atop the brick fireplace foot using a toilet paper roll for a microphone. She would join the scene in a moment. But right now she needed to settle a matter.

She was tired of lobbing blame at God for all of the wars fought between herself and her dad. He had changed. So had she. He had even cancelled a board meeting to take her out for seafood on St. Pete Beach. Things were different now between Dad and herself. But she had to take the time to do for God what her father had done for her: spend time alone with him.

One knee went to the carpet. Since before her college days, she had carried rejection inside herself like a sickness. She crouched and lifted her hand. The warmth of the candles glowed beneath her fingertips.

"I don't have the right to do this, but I need you now, Father, your forgiveness, your mercy, and your touch. . . ."

20

ABOVE THE SHELTER for homeless women and children in Tampa Bay, the streetlights blazed through a fog that settled over the ocean-side city, tall iron poles that stood like rows of lighthouses encircled with garlands and large red plastic ribbons. The holiday lights inside of the mission windows glittered and blinked like eyes, new white lights that winked at the crowd gathered along the walk. A crew of church people had installed the Christmas lights along with a twenty-foot-tall tree that shadowed the lobby entrance with branches and paper ornaments that shuddered whenever the front door opened. Twenty-six children, all festooned with angel wings and halos woven with silver-star tinsel, emptied several large boxes brimming with wrapped gifts.

Wade and Isabella Jenkins helped the church children place the gifts beneath the tree while the displaced mothers and children followed Nora Maggert and Grace Huddleston to the rows of folding chairs where the families took their seats.

Sam Farris stroked the side of his face and watched the choir members file into the mission to take their places on the risers. "We've never done it this way, Pastor."

"I know, Sam." Wade joined Sam while Isabella finished up with the Christmas angels project.

"Some of the older folk don't understand." Sam directed the remainder of the choir toward the risers.

"They will. If not here tonight, then later. In heaven."

"I've heard a few folks say the pageant should stay within the four walls of the church. Let these people come to us, they say," said Sam.

"Do they now, Sam? Can't please everyone, I guess. But look at Nora and Grace. I've never seen them so lit up."

"They do shine like two new pennies. Your daughter, Sydney, she's really taken an interest in this mission."

"This was her idea, Sam."

"That women's group she just started on Thursday nights, they say it's an awfully curious group."

"It's a Bible study, Sam. Nothing curious about it."

"Except all the women are—were—women of ill repute, that is to say—"

"Prostitutes, Sam. Sydney has started a Bible study for the women she's met out here on the streets."

Sam surveyed the crowd. "Are some of them here tonight?"

SYDNEY KNELT at a folding chair in a ten-by-thirteen-foot room, a corner of the shelter used for overflow donations but emptied on this night by Sydney and her girls. The murmured prayers of the six other women she had collected from the streets of downtown Tampa illumined her heart even more than the large blue candle on a corner stand lit up the room.

A mission volunteer opened the door. "Ms. Oliver, they're ready for you."

Sydney felt a hand on hers, that of a woman of eighteen named Sherry.

"I hope I look all right," said Sherry. "Praying makes me cry."

"You look nice, Sherry. Nice dress," said Sydney. "We have to go, everyone. Look for Grace Huddleston. She saved you all a seat. See you all at the reception afterwards."

"Are you nervous?" asked Sherry.

"No. As long as I remember that what we're doing isn't about me."

"But it is about you, Sydney. I was a sicko, but look at me now."

"It's your faith that's made you well, Sherry."

"They're playing music. Go on, now. They need you," said Sherry. Each woman hugged Sydney.

⌣

"IT'S TIME TO START, maestro. Your audience is ready," Wade said to Sam. He escorted Isabella, followed by Trevor and Allie, to the front row. Sydney joined them.

"It's so good to have everyone home this year," said Isabella. "Reminds me of the year we were all in Tennessee in the mountains."

"No snow," said Wade. "Otherwise, yes, it's like that."

"Trevor, you and Allie sit here next to Grammy," said Sydney. "Daddy, have you heard anything from New Orleans?"

"Corette and Pierre have agreed to cooperate with the police. That's not good news for Reverend DeLucey. DeLucey's trying to rally his supporters. Looks like he'll spend the rest of his days trying to save himself instead of his followers. Corette may get off altogether for cooperating. And the fact that Pierre turned himself in is in his favor. They are taking into consideration that he helped nail a dealer they've been trying to nab. I told him that he and I should have a few more chats."

"Pierre agreed to that?" Sydney asked.

"He did."

"Daddy, you're amazing."

"Thank you, honey."

"They're ready, Sydney," said Isabella.

Sydney stood and ascended the small temporary platform erected by the pageant set crew. "We're so glad you all could come. This night is electrified with the Christmas spirit, and I hope that if you don't sense it now, that you will before you leave."

"Can you believe our shy daughter?" asked Isabella.

"She just needed the right audience."

"Makes a good narrator, Sam says," said Isabella.

"Better her than me."

"I mailed off those clothes you picked out, sent them off to that New Orleans mission, Wade. Bye-bye, yellow shirt."

"You're a good wife, Isabella. I want Mr. Frances to have those nice shirts."

"Oh, he's that angel you told me about. I sure started rumors with that little piece of news about your Christmas angel."

"Doesn't matter. As long as they believe."

Suzie and Buzz, representing Mary and Joseph, walked quietly to the rear of the mission to take their places. Wade sighed. It had been a tough decision to marry those two against his better judgment. But God's grace makes up for past mistakes. He knew that better than anyone else.

"Wade!" Isabella gasped and pointed at the window.

Wade followed her eyes. "It's Lance. They did make it, by george!" He patted Isabella's leg. "You stay here with the kids. I'll bring them in."

Out on the sidewalk, Wade embraced his son and daughter-in-law and their three children. The choir commenced a chorus of "Joy to the World" while the church orchestra resounded with brass and percussion. Other families came in from off the streets until the mission was filled to capacity.

Wade felt a biting cold kiss upon his cheek. "We better get inside. It's misting out here."

"Look, Dad!" Lance pointed toward the streetlights. The illumined aura around the lamps filled with light flakes that fluttered and swirled to the pavement. "I can't believe it. Snow in Tampa Bay."

"Isabella always gets her way," Wade said.

SYDNEY STEPPED ASIDE while the choir sang. Through the window she saw her brother and father.

"Go on, Sydney, go to them," Isabella whispered. "The choir has two more verses to go."

Sydney stepped out into the halo of light just outside the mission door. She tugged on her father's coattail. "You didn't tell me."

"Oh. Sydney, your brother's coming for Christmas," said Wade.

"Was that the scaredy-cat on the platform?" Lance kissed her cheek.

"We'll need more coats for the mission, Daddy," said Sydney.

"I'll make a note of it." Wade directed Lance's wife and kids through the door.

Sydney knew that Pastor Wade Jenkins was a different sort of shepherd now—a different sort of man. Some liked the new Wade Jenkins. Some didn't. But everyone agreed that Christmas had a new spirit about it that year. While a lost snow cloud from Maine had taken a wrong turn in Jersey and wound up in Tampa Bay, a father had taken a wrong turn in the Big Easy and wound up with his family.

Sydney always felt that on that December night, the angels must have kissed the sky with hope or magic—or both. She imagined that as the orchestra struck up the first notes that night, the angels must have danced all over the powdery streets dressed as ragged men and women with needy hearts. Not every person can see an angel disguised as one in need.

As Wade turned to go inside, Sydney tugged at the hem of his jacket. "May I have this dance?" she asked.

"Can we dance to 'Joy to the World'?"

"Anything is possible, Daddy. It's Christmas."

The old-timers later told Sydney that it had never snowed in

Tampa Bay until this night. She was quick to tell anyone who asked that whenever they heard about the year it snowed in Tampa, they should consider themselves privy to the biggest miracle to come into the city that night. God can make it snow in the blink of an eye, she would always tell them. But to change a stubborn heart takes a miracle beyond human imagination. All it took from him . . . was one touch.

about the author

Patricia Hickman is an award-winning novelist, a part-time speaker, a pastor's wife, and a mother. Her other books include *Sand Pebbles, Katrina's Wings,* and *Fallen Angels,* the first book in her upcoming series. Patricia's novels have received critical acclaim and earned her multiple awards, including two Silver Angel Awards for Excellence in Media. She loves gardening, picnicking with her family, and working in the church she and her husband founded in North Carolina. You may find out more information about Patricia Hickman and her other works by visiting her Web site at www.patriciahickman.com. The author welcomes you to e-mail her at the Web site and share your comments.

about the artist

A Christian, cleverly disguised as an artist, Ron DiCianni has been a professional illustrator for nearly thirty years, commissioned by some of the world's largest companies.

In the last decade Ron has felt the inspiration to communicate godly principles through his work, considering art more communication than decoration. As a result of yielding his talent back to the Lord, he has been privileged to be in the forefront of the crusade for "Reclaiming the arts for Christ," through a Second Renaissance.

This "crusade" has included forming The MasterPeace Collection with DaySpring, conceiving and coauthoring the best-selling Tell Me series with Max Lucado, Joni Eareckson Tada, and Michael Card, as well as his solo efforts *Beyond Words* and *Travels of Messenger*, with his sons, both published by Tyndale. He has also been the cover artist for such best-selling books as *This Present Darkness, Piercing the Darkness,* and *Angelwalk.*

Most recently he has launched Art2see, a company devoted to proclaiming Christ through a variety of artistic venues, to both the Christian and secular markets through his company's partnership with Somerset Publishing in Houston.

DiCianni and his wife, Pat, live in Buffalo Grove, Illinois. They consider their two greatest works of art to be their sons, Grant, a paramedic and firefighter, and Warren, a YWAM student currently in Perth, Australia, becoming the man of God he was born to be.

a note from the artist

My mission is not to make Scripture relevant. It is to show that it already is and always will be. Patty Hickman demonstrates through powerful writing that reaching the hem of Jesus' garment was not a onetime event, but an example and invitation to make it happen at every needful moment of our lives. Jesus' hem is but a touch away. It is only for you to reach out.

You have no doubt often heard it said, "One picture is worth a thousand words." In the case of these novellas we decided to bring it to reality.

Each of these handsomely crafted stories is meant to bring you an experience of words and picture, which has been a lost art to many. I believe that's what Oswald Chambers alluded to when he said,

"We have lost our power to visualize. . . ."

There is a world of truth in that statement. We hope that these will set you on the road to visualize and engage the use of your imagination as you allow these stories to indelibly impact your mind with the eternal truths of God's word. Allow yourself to dream and wonder and be immersed in the story, because each one is about the human condition. Each one is about you.

I'm privileged to have a small part in each of these. I hope that together the words and pictures will remain with you forever.

Ron DiCianni